REVENGE is Sweet

Three houses, three couples—three reasons for revenge

The calm ambience of St. Fiacre's Hill— where lavish homes provided a secure haven for the seriously rich—hid a maelstrom of feeling. Geraint Howell-Williams, Triss Alexander and Dominic Dashwood all thought they had a need to avenge—but the actions each set in motion gained a steamroller life of their own, with entirely unexpected results.

GETTING EVEN is the first book in Sharon Kendrick's REVENGE IS SWEET trilogy. Look out for Triss's story coming next month in KISS AND TELL (#1951), and Dominic's story, SETTLING THE SCORE (#1957), is out in May.

Dear Reader,

"Revenge is a dish best served cold."

The above line grabbed my attention the very first time I read it. Revenge is a strong, deep emotion—passion with a dark, sometimes bitter, side to it—and I have chosen it as the linking theme for my St. Fiacre's books.

I like the idea of my characters—all outwardly highly successful people—having a secret side to their natures. A side that can plot to avenge themselves, a side that might sometimes appall them, but that they are powerless to resist—for the darkest emotions are always the most irresistible....

What motivates revenge? It is always the sense of having been wronged, a chance to win after an earlier defeat. And like all deep, controlling passions, revenge has a knock-on effect.

But don't take my word for it—find out yourself from Geraint, Triss and Dominic....

Sharon Kendrick

SHARON KENDRICK

Getting Even

Harlequin Books

TORONTO • NEW YORK • LONDON
AMSTERDAM • PARIS • SYDNEY • HAMBURG
STOCKHOLM • ATHENS • TOKYO • MILAN
MADRID • WARSAW • BUDAPEST • AUCKLAND

ISBN 0-373-11945-3

GETTING EVEN

First North American Publication 1998.

CHAPTER ONE

'PINCH me, quick! Who the hell *is* he?'

'No idea—but just watch me find out!'

Lola, who had been shamelessly listening in to this conversation, watched as the two women tottered across the clubhouse towards the object of their desire.

And then her heart missed a beat. Or rather it missed several.

Lola blinked as the man glanced up and looked at her. And just carried on looking.

It was the classic, corny situation—the kind that Lola had read about in books and had never really believed could happen.

Well, it was happening now, and to *her*! Eyes meeting across a crowded room and all the things that went with it whether you liked it or not—the heightened awareness and the not so subtle body language which shrieked out mutual attraction.

Lola recognised him immediately. But he wouldn't recognise *her*; of that she was certain. People never did! Lola was an air stewardess, and once she changed out of her uniform she was anonymous—it went hand in hand with the job!

She swallowed, unable to tear her eyes away from him.

As well as being the most outrageously attractive man in the room, he was making no effort to disguise his rather bored indifference. With eyes like

5

storm clouds he was moodily surveying the proceedings as if he would rather be somewhere else.

Well, you and me both, buddy, thought Lola, with a touch of defiance!

She usually adored parties—the fact that she was invited to so many was one of the perks of her job with the airline—but this party was slightly different.

For a start she knew no one.

Everyone seemed to be standing around in large, impenetrable groups which didn't look particularly welcoming. And she didn't really feel like going up to one of them and saying in her best stewardess voice, 'Hi, I'm Lola—who are you?'

The man with the stormy eyes was in the middle of just such a clique, and a scrumptious-looking blonde who had clearly poured herself into her black, sequinned dress without much thought of how she was going to get out of it was gazing into his eyes as if all her Christmases had come at once. And she wasn't the only one. He seemed to have that hypnotic effect on just about every female in the room.

Lola could see exactly why.

He wasn't precisely what you'd call *good-*looking, she decided, not in a boring, even-featured sort of way. His nose looked as though it had been broken—probably on the rugby field, thought Lola as she took in the broad, strong shoulders. But the imperfection only seemed to add to the rather devastating overall attractiveness of his face.

His mouth was sublime—he had the most sensual lips that Lola had ever seen—but there was an unmistakably hard, almost cruel curve to its corners which hinted at a powerful, sexual mastery which Lola loathed herself for finding attractive.

His shoulders were broad, as she had already noted, and his legs were long, and you could sense, rather than see, that every muscle in his hard-packed, spectacular body had been honed to perfection.

This was no rich, pretty boy, thought Lola, with the sense of being in the presence of someone remarkable; this was a *real* man—tough and strong and uncompromising. Unwillingly, she felt the first faint stirrings of desire.

The man glanced up from listening to the blonde bombshell who was now whispering excitedly into his ear, and, much to Lola's fury, caught her watching him again.

He raised one quizzical black brow in a look which somehow managed to be both insulting and yet captivating, and Lola angrily stared down into her glass, which contained nothing more exciting than tonic water with a piece of lemon bobbing around in it.

Arrogant so-and-so! she thought disparagingly. And you are *not* to look at him again. He's the kind of man who will misinterpret even *one* look—and have you down under his favourite category: easily seduced!

The buzz of party conversation, fuelled by ever increasing amounts of alcohol, was gradually getting louder and louder. More for something to do than because she was interested in the music, Lola moved towards the front of the stage, where the band who had been hired for the evening were now tuning up, and wondered how soon she could politely make her escape.

She had been awake since five a.m. this morning, and had only arrived back from Vienna an hour ago. Common sense made her wonder why she had bothered to come at all.

Simple. She had come because she had been invited by the Residents' Association of the plush St Fiacre's Hill estate.

St Fiacre's Hill was *the* most amazing place to live, and she herself, unbelievably, was now a resident there—thanks to the totally unexpected generosity of one of Lola's airline passengers who had taken a great big shine to her—and left her a house on one of the most exclusive developments in England!

She had come tonight because even after six months of living there she still did not really feel part of the luxury estate, and because sometimes she suspected that she never would.

But one thing was certain—she never *would* fit in if she shunned the events which studded the busy St Fiacre's social calendar.

Which was why she was standing awkwardly and alone in the ultra-plush clubhouse, wishing that she were safely tucked up at home in bed. Alone!

A pretty boring ambition for a twenty-five-year-old, she thought wryly as she took another sip of tonic, then winced because it tasted flat and stale.

'That looks as if it could do with a new lease of life,' came a deep-voiced, confident observation from just behind Lola's left shoulder, and she knew without looking that it was the man with the stormy grey eyes.

She forced herself to turn slowly, to meet what turned out to be a predictably mocking gaze, and gave him a steady and deliberate 'You-don't-impress-*me*' kind of look, though in this case it was difficult because the man exuded a kind of earthy sensuality which made Lola's breath catch in the back of her throat.

In her job as a flight attendant, she met gorgeous men every single day of her life—although, admittedly, they weren't usually this gorgeous. Men who had women eating out of their hands like pussycats. Men whom Lola avoided like the plague. Men like this equalled heartbreak!

'What does?' she answered rather coolly, just as the lead guitarist chose that moment to break one of his strings. 'The guitar?'

He shot her a deadpan look. 'Actually, I'm clean out of guitar strings,' he murmured, in the most amazing voice that Lola had ever heard—it was soft and deep and dark, with an attractive, almost musical lilt underlying it. 'But no, that wasn't what I had in mind.'

Something about the clean-cut sensuality of his mouth affected Lola in a very frightening and fundamental way. She felt tiny shivers of awareness skate tingling little pathways across her skin, and such a primitive, physical response to a man she did not know brought all her self-protective instincts to the fore.

In her job she observed human nature at close quarters most days and she knew that predatory men were intimidated by women who gave as good as they got. Even so, it still took an effort to make her voice stay calm as she said, 'And just what *did* you have in mind?' Which was, of course, the very *worst* thing she could have said!

'Oughtn't we at least be introduced before I start propositioning you?' he mocked, the mouth hardening into a sexy line.

So he *didn't* recognize her! He had no recollection of her bending forward, with her brightest smile, to put his drink down in front of him on the aircraft table.

For some reason, Lola felt slightly let down by this. There was nothing so insulting as not being noticed!

Ignoring the proposition bit, she held her hand out towards him. 'Lola Hennessy,' she said as evenly as she could, which was a bit difficult when confronted by that thoughtful stare.

'Lola,' he said slowly, and took the proffered hand in a firm grasp that felt quite wonderful. 'Is that your real name?'

Lola shook her dark head. It was, at least, an improvement on the usual comment—most people assumed she had been named after the pop song! 'I was christened Dolores.'

He nodded. 'Yes,' he murmured. 'Lola is the pet form, isn't it? So is Lolita.' His grey gaze was ironic as his deep voice caressed the word. 'Do they never call you Lolita?'

She gave him a steady look. 'Lolita was a fictional nymphet,' she answered acidly. 'Are you trying to make a point?'

'No, I'm not,' he drawled, mocking amusement lighting the depths of the stormy eyes. 'And besides, you're a little too old to be classified as nymphet, aren't you?'

It was hardly surprising, in the circumstances, that she should blush, and blushing only added to the feeling of intense vulnerability which had been present since he had first started talking to her. However, at least Lola had a pale olive tint to her skin, which masked the colour far more than a classic English rose complexion would have done.

'Yes,' she answered shortly, and tried to freeze him with an angry look which would have had a lesser man scuttling off in the opposite direction. 'Much too old.'

But he seemed unmoved by her embarrassment, and uncaring of her anger—and instead allowed a grey gaze that was now cool rather than stormy to rove speculatively over her.

'And you look like a Dolores,' he remarked suddenly. 'With that mane of curly brown-black hair and skin which looks as creamy as the best cappuccino. But your eyes should be dark, shouldn't they? Mysterious and black. Yet yours are blue. Bright blue. The blue of a Mediterranean sky.'

Lola met many men in her job, but she had never met anyone who was quite so self-assured as *this* man—and she found herself stung into defence. 'I'm an odd mixture,' she found herself telling him. 'Mum says she doesn't know where I get it from.' And then she looked down to discover that he was still holding onto her fingertips, in a parody of a handshake!

His grey eyes followed the direction of her gaze, to where her hand lay so acquiescently against his. 'And what else are you going to tell me about yourself, Lola Hennessy—other than the fact that the touch of my hand makes yours tremble with awareness—?'

Furiously, she snatched her hand away. 'Or revulsion, perhaps?'

He laughed. 'I don't think so. Unless your eyes are lying, of course.'

She pretended to consider this, both invigorated and unsettled by the game she was allowing herself to play. 'And do you think that is possible?' she queried. 'For the eyes to be able to lie?'

'I don't just think so, I know so. Deception is an art which can be learned through practice just like any other.'

Lola felt like a child who had tentatively dipped her toe into a puddle and become submerged right up to her neck. 'There speaks a true cynic,' she observed caustically.

He shrugged his wide shoulders, and a look of faint surprise crossed the dark, handsome face. 'I'm thirty-four,' he stated, with an air of finality. 'Therefore I am a cynic.'

Lola laughed nervously as she mentally worked out that he was nine years older than she was. 'And why should that follow?'

His eyes were smoky with a kind of regret. 'Because I have seen enough of life, and of women, to know that there are few surprises left. But even cynics are interested in young women who send out such mixed messages. Or should I say *especially* cynics...?'

His voice held a slumberous quality now, and to her horror Lola found herself imagining what that voice would sound like first thing in the morning, all husky and heavy with sleep.

'And do I?' she ventured boldly. 'Send out mixed messages?'

'Most certainly you do.'

'How?' she asked, even though something inside her urged her to walk away from him. Before he snared her completely in the silken bonds of his charm.

He lowered his voice, as if he recognised that the question had been unwise. 'You recognise the danger in me, and you want to dislike me—even, perhaps, hate me,' he stated huskily. 'But you can't quite bring yourself to, can you, Lola?'

And he was absolutely right, damn him! Lola adopted the unstressed, unflappable smile she usually reserved for passengers who had been hitting the duty-free in a big way. 'Why on earth should I want to dislike you?'

The laughter which had lurked at the depths of the grey eyes disappeared and Lola was taken aback by how hard his face suddenly looked. And how cold. 'I have absolutely no idea,' he answered slowly, and his eyes narrowed into cool, granite chips.

Lola registered that her heart was racing, that the blood was thundering in her head in a most uncomfortable and unwelcome way. What would he do, she wondered, if she told him that the reason why she was reacting so bizarrely and so uniquely was because at the ripe old age of twenty-five she was experiencing an overwhelming desire to be in his arms and to have him crush his mouth down on hers?

Lola shivered, acknowledging her relative inexperience with men, despite working in the seemingly glamorous air travel industry.

Oh, she had been attracted to men in the past—of course she had. She had even come very close to having a proper love-affair. But she had never experienced feelings like this before. These dark, powerful, grown-up stirrings were a whole new and rather frightening ball game.

And she could not have chosen a worse candidate to be wildly attracted to—a rich, arrogant, gorgeous cynic! Lola was not an idiot, and she knew without someone having to tell her that this man was way, *way* out of her reach!

His voice had now dropped to a velvet caress. 'So tell me, Lola Hennessy, just why you dislike me so.'

Sure! And boost his already massive ego still further? She was full of tricks like that! Lola gave him a bemused stare before delivering a gentle put-down. 'How could I possibly dislike you, for heaven's sake? I don't even *know* you.'

Had he guessed that her indifference was feigned? Was that why his stormy eyes were now sending out shadowy messages which made another shiver of foreboding tiptoe its way up Lola's spine?

'Well, that's one thing that is easily remedied,' he replied silkily. 'I'm Geraint Howell-Williams,' he said, and his slate-grey eyes narrowed by a fraction as he waited for her reaction.

He was obviously *someone*, thought Lola—that much was evident just from his appearance—but did that infinitesimal pause after he had introduced himself mean she should have heard of him?

Arrogant so-and-so! Even if she *had* heard of him she would have pretended not to have! 'How do you do, Mr Howell-Williams?' she responded, her reply coming out all wooden and formal, and she saw his mouth harden very briefly before dazzling her with the most transfixing smile that Lola had ever encountered.

There was a hint of wicked amusement lurking in the depths of those eyes now. 'Oh, call me Geraint, please,' he murmured.

'If you insist,' she answered stiffly.

'I wouldn't *dream* of insisting,' he mocked softly. 'I've always found persuasion to be a much more effective tool.'

Now that she could believe! One more dazzling smile like the one he had displayed earlier and Lola could easily imagine being persuaded into doing almost anything he wanted...

'I'm sure you have,' she said softly, a wry note to her voice, and their eyes met for a moment of complete understanding, which left Lola feeling slightly shaken...

He threw her a thoughtful look. 'This is some building,' he commented slowly, as if determined to put the conversation back on a more conventional footing.

'Yes, it is.' Lola dutifully looked around the clubhouse, taking in the high white moulded ceiling and the pale marble pillars which gleamed so discreetly. On each pillar was mounted the distinctive navy blue St Fiacre's crest, lavishly embossed with golden dragons and unicorns and vine leaves.

'It looks less like a tennis club and more like a Greek temple—and an exceptionally sumptuous

temple, to boot!' Lola observed rather drily. 'It
must have cost an absolute fortune to build!'

'I'm sure it did. But this is, after all, St Fiacre's,'
he observed rather drily. 'Where fortunes are ten-
a-penny.'

'You sound as if you don't approve,' she commented curiously.

'Do I?' He gave a brief shake of his dark head
before fixing her with a steady look. 'I was simply
making an observation,' he demurred softly. 'Not
a value judgement. If I disapproved of wealth and
its occasional excesses, then I wouldn't be here tonight, now would I?'

'I suppose not,' answered Lola, wondering what
it was about him that made her skin alternately hot
and cold as she veered between finding him dis-
tinctly dangerous and finding him almost irresistible—which was far more worrying!

'So, Lola . . .' he smiled ' . . . now that we have the
formalities out of the way, what would you like to
do next? Eat?'

Before he had breezed over, Lola's stomach had
been rumbling loud enough to rival the London
Philharmonic Orchestra, but now, astonishingly, it
was silent. And her appetite had completely deserted her.

A first indeed! Perhaps if she stayed in this man's
company for long enough she might be able to zip
up her black skirt before next Christmas!

'I'm not hungry,' she said.

'Oh, Lo-la, you disappoint me,' he drawled
softly. 'One of the things that makes you stand out
from all the other women in this room is that you
look as though you really take pleasure in eating.'

Lola glowered. 'There's no need to make me sound like a strapping great beast of the fields!'

He laughed. 'That wasn't my intention at all.' His grey eyes flicked briefly over her body. 'I'm sure that enough men have commented favourably on those *lus-cious* curves before me.'

There it was again. That lilting and unsettling way he had of addressing her—Lola couldn't quite make out whether that last remark had been an insult or not. Or what the way he looked at her actually *meant*. It was as though he couldn't quite make up his mind whether to dislike her or to...to...

Lola shook her head to rid herself of the horrifyingly erotic vision which had crept into her mind, which involved a lot of very old-fashioned macho behaviour, such as Geraint Howell-Williams throwing her over his shoulder, and then, then...

Besides, he should *not* make comments like that to someone he had never met before. Well, they *had* met, when she had served him with drinks *en route* to Paris a couple of weeks ago, but clearly he did not, as she had anticipated, remember her.

Being an air hostess was a bit like being a nurse— you all looked pretty much the same in uniform! And the passenger who had chatted away to you quite happily during a flight would usually stare at you blankly if you encountered him or her outside the confines of the craft or airport.

The surprising thing was that it usually worked the other way round, too, and Lola rarely recognised her passengers once they were off the aircraft.

But Geraint Howell-Williams was different. You would not need to be a genius to acknowledge that he was the type of man who, once seen, would never be forgotten . . .

Lola's eyes glittered. 'Actually, no,' she contradicted him now icily. 'Men do not usually comment on my figure, curves or otherwise. For a start, I don't encourage personal remarks—'

'Don't you?' he mocked softly. 'Then what a shockingly boring life you must have led.' His grey eyes locked with hers in an irresistible and yet somehow disquieting challenge.

'I agree!' she returned, with a sweet smile. 'And standing here talking to you is just about as boring as it can get!'

Lola watched as for one swift, disconcerting moment his eyes darkened with an intensity of emotion which puzzled her hugely. She had made him angry, yes. Had she managed to wound his pride too? And, if so, might he at least now have the grace to look a little apologetic?

No way, she quickly realised. The anger had vanished, and so had the dark, intense look. And surprisingly all that was left was laughter—a reluctant kind of laughter which lurked in the depths of his grey eyes.

'I don't believe I bore you, Lola,' he told her softly. 'I believe that boredom is the very last thing on your mind right now!'

Oh, the arrogance of the man! Lola might have laughed if she hadn't been so outraged by his inflated opinion of himself! 'You find that such an improbable concept, do you?' she queried coolly. 'That a woman should find you boring?'

'I do when she is demonstrating all the obvious signs of sexual attraction,' he mused.

'That's probably just wishful thinking on your part!' retorted Lola instantly, then wished she hadn't.

He smiled, but it was the kind of smile that all the bad guys in films possessed—it didn't make the corners of his eyes go all crinkly, and it didn't have any degree of warmth in it either. Again, Lola felt that uncomfortable chill creep across the surface of her skin.

'Is it? Does wishful thinking manage to manufacture eyes which keep darkening with passion, or lips that automatically soften and part in anticipation of being kissed?' he drawled silkily. 'As yours are doing right now?'

To her horror, Lola suddenly felt absolutely weak with longing as the deep, sensual words seemed to orchestrate her response. The fairly sensible, middle-of-the-road woman she considered herself to be had suddenly been replaced by a pathetic, swooning *wimp*! 'St-stop it,' she implored, despising herself for sounding so feeble but unable to do anything about it.

He shook his dark head. 'But you don't want me to stop it, do you? That's just the trouble. You like it, Lola. And you like me. Your body is telling me just how much, isn't it?'

And his eyes lazily flicked over her, lingering with undisguised interest on her breasts in a way that Lola would have found intolerable if any other man had done it. But she did not find it intolerable when Geraint Howell-Williams did it.

Beneath the dress of lapis lazuli velvet which made her blue eyes even bluer, Lola could feel her body betraying her, flowering beneath the approbation and the hunger in his eyes. She felt her breasts grow heavy and full, the tips begin to prickle with a kind of delicious ache which was actually more uncomfortable than enjoyable.

Because Lola recognised that there was only one way of taking that terrible aching away and that, astonishingly and shockingly, she wanted Geraint to touch her...

'Do you normally behave like this towards women you have only just met?' she demanded, her knees now weak with wanting.

'Never,' he responded softly, clearly mesmerised by the jutting thrust of her breasts against the rich material of her dress. 'Do you normally react in this way to men you have only just met?'

Lola dragged a deep, determined breath into her lungs. 'I think I'd better get out of here,' she told him breathlessly. 'Before one of us says something *really* offensive—'

'You're in no state to go anywhere,' he responded wryly as he looked down at her searchingly, the stormy eyes narrowing in surprise at her wide eyes and flushed face. 'Here, give me that.'

'That' was the glass she was clutching as if it were a lifeline, and smoothly—masterfully—he managed to remove the forgotten tonic from her hand and deposit it on a nearby table, then slowly pull her into his arms before she had time to make a protest.

'Geraint, please...' she whispered, aware of a tiny pull of pleasure as she said his name for the first time, and she found herself wanting to say it over and over again, as though it were some life-sustaining mantra.

'Please what?' he responded softly, his mouth pressed against her hair.

'Please let go of me.'

'If I do you'll fall.' His voice deepened. 'Won't you?'

'N-no, I won't,' she answered uncertainly, realising that she was actually enjoying the rather scary feeling of being this much out of control.

'Try it,' he suggested, and loosened his hands from where they had been holding her by the waist, and Lola actually felt herself sway, like a flu victim just out of bed for the first time. She wondered if she might have slithered to the floor, had he not renewed his hold on her with a steely strength that made Lola feel weaker than she had ever felt in her life.

'See?' he challenged softly.

Oh, yes, Lola saw all right. She saw that she had been sending out entirely the wrong messages to Geraint Howell-Williams since she had first clapped eyes on him tonight.

Or maybe—just maybe—she had been sending out the *right* messages, and he was just clever enough to pick up on them, realise that she was hopelessly infatuated, and then capitalise on that by having her almost swooning in his arms.

'Relax,' he urged softly. 'Just enjoy the music.'

For a moment she did as he suggested. She gave in to temptation and to feeling, loving the exciting warm circle of his arms, the way his head rested so easily against hers.

She forgot all about the band playing and listened to the infinitely more spellbinding music of his body.

The beat of his heart. The rhythm of his breathing. The almost unconscious little thrust of his pelvis as he allowed himself to respond to the saxophonist who was the band's only saving grace.

She knew that she ought to move, that a dance with a stranger should not be this intimate, and yet, to all intents and purposes, the dance was *not* intimate. They were just a man and a woman swaying loosely in each other's arms, as others were all around them.

So this sensation of almost drowning in sweet, drenching pleasure—was this unique to her? Did this dance feel like any other to Geraint Howell-Williams? Lola wondered. Because it sure as hell didn't to her! At that moment, drifting in his arms, she felt as though she was starring in every love story ever written.

Love story?

Her adolescent little fantasies brought Lola back to her senses with a start, and as the number trailed off with one final, lingering throb of the saxophone she took a deep breath and looked up at him.

'Th-thank you for the dance,' she said falteringly.

The grey eyes were enigmatic as he dropped his hands from where they had been lightly holding her hips. 'My pleasure.'

'It's time I was going.'

'Sure?'

That was, thought Lola wryly, what they called a leading question. To be honest, she wasn't sure— she would have liked to hang around and dance like that with him all night.

But a girl had her pride to think of. He was the kind of over-gorgeous man who had probably had things much, *much* too easy in the past. And Lola's turning him down was almost certainly going to help his emotional development enormously! 'Quite sure,' she answered firmly.

He nodded his dark head. 'Where do you live?'

Lola had only been a resident for the past six months, and she still had not worked out how to answer this particular question without giving in to the toe-curling embarrassment of having to explain how she'd actually come to own a house worth almost a million pounds.

People always jumped to such awful conclusions when they found out that a pensioner she hardly knew had left it to her!

'I live here,' she told him. 'On the St Fiacre's estate.'

'I see,' he murmured softly.

Lola searched his face for the tell-tale looks of surprise—but there were none.

She was still extremely sensitive about living in a house on the estate once termed 'the Beverly Hills of England' by some enterprising journalist—one where all the residents were not just rich, they were *seriously* rich.

Except for Lola, of course.

The rich had a look and a lifestyle all of their own, and Lola did not possess either! She looked exactly what she was—a working woman who needed a bit of clever juggling to pay her bills. Although, admittedly, a working woman who lived in an enormous house. A house which she was fast coming to the conclusion she was going to have to sell.

'I'll walk you back,' he said.

'No!' It came out more vehemently than she had
intended, but *really*! A walk home in the moonlight with a man like Geraint Howell-Williams?
Agreeing to a dream scenario like that would simply
be asking for trouble!

'And why not?' he asked coolly.

He was very persistent, she would say that for
him, although she doubted that he had ever had to
use persistence with a woman before! 'Does there
have to be a reason?' she parried. 'Or are you implying that no woman in her right mind would
refuse an invitation to have you walk her home?'

He fixed her with a steady grey gaze. 'Did you
come here with another man tonight?'

'Do you think that I would have been dancing
like that with *you* if I had come with another man?'
Lola demanded, instantly growing flustered. Now
why had she mentioned the way they had been
dancing—especially when it made his eyes gleam
with such a hot, exciting look?

'I have no idea.' He shrugged shoulders whose
breadth was emphasised by the exquisite cut of his
dinner jacket. 'Who knows what hidden agenda a
woman might have when she agrees to dance with
a man?'

Or vice versa, thought Lola with amusement.
'Such as?'

He plucked two glasses of champagne from the
tray of a passing waitress and handed one to Lola
who took it without thinking. 'Such as wanting to
show off her figure in a clinging gown. That could
easily apply to you . . .'

Lola, who had not intended to drink alcohol at
all that evening, now took a huge, emboldening slug

of the fizzy wine and was grateful for the warmth and the bravado it gave her. 'This dress is *not* clinging!' she declared, glancing down at the deep blue velvet.

There was smoky amusement in the grey eyes. 'Oh, come on, Lola,' he chided softly. 'It probably wasn't *meant* to be—but when you combine a sensual material like velvet with a Botticelli body clinging is what you get.'

'You mean I look fat?'

'I mean you look sensational,' he murmured, sounding as though he meant it. 'If you really want to know.'

Lola felt a rush of pleasure kick-starting at the pit of her stomach. This man whom she was trying so hard to dislike was flirting like mad with her, and right now she didn't care!

Flustered, she swept a great handful of hair unnecessarily over her shoulder. 'And what other reasons do women have for dancing with men?' she queried, in an effort to stop him giving her that hungry look which was making her long to be kissed by him.

'To make a boyfriend jealous, perhaps?'

'But I haven't got a boyfriend,' said Lola instantly, and then could have kicked herself. There was no need to make herself sound as though she was desperate! Or on the shelf. Or *both*! 'Not at the moment, anyway,' she finished defiantly.

'No,' he said thoughtfully.

Lola found herself wishing that she could check her appearance somewhere. Was her nose shiny? Had her mascara smudged beneath her eyes? Was that why he was subjecting her to that highly disturbing, narrow-eyed scrutiny?

'And there is, of course,' he drawled, 'the rather obvious reason why a woman agrees to dance with a man.'

'And what's that?'

'Oh, I think you know the answer to that one.' He gave her a long, steady look.

Lola took the look as a challenge. 'No, I don't.'

The grey eyes glittered. 'That she can't resist him, of course. That she wants to be in bed with him . . . and dancing is a socially acceptable substitute for sex. Sublimation,' he finished on a mocking note, and then, as if sensing her objection, added softly, 'You *did* ask, Lola.'

He was right. Perhaps it had been naïve of her. But then again, there were civilised ways of answering naïve questions, weren't there? The glass froze halfway to Lola's lips. 'Are you trying to shock me?'

'Why?' he mocked, and their gazes locked for a fraught and sexually charged moment. 'Am I succeeding?'

Not in shocking her, no—he was *exciting* her by saying things he had no right to be saying. It was crazy, thought Lola, how a deep voice and a sexy body could turn a normally sensible girl's brain to jelly! 'No comment!' she declared firmly. 'And I'm definitely going now!'

'Did you drive?'

'No, I walked.'

'Then I am going to walk you home,' he said, and shook his dark head firmly as he saw her open her mouth to refuse. 'Please, Lola,' he urged, almost huskily. 'It's a dark night for a woman to be out on her own.'

It was years since a man had said something so delightfully chivalrous to her, although Lola usually associated chivalry with a certain kind of innocence—and innocence was not a word which suited Geraint Howell-Williams at all!

She tipped her chin up to look him in the eye, so that her hair spilled down in mahogany spirals all over her shoulders. 'And which, out of interest, offers me more in the way of danger?' she challenged. 'The dark night? Or you?'

'You're talking different types of danger, honey,' he asserted, giving her a brief, hard smile—but it was an oddly disconcerting smile. 'Though I can assure you that I will deliver you home in one piece. Does that satisfy you?'

It occurred to Lola that 'satisfy' was a particularly poor word to have chosen in the circumstances, but she nodded as he put their glasses down on one of the tables and guided her towards the door like a man used to being in command.

She felt her heart racing out of control. Calm down, Lola, she told herself firmly—he's only offering to walk you home, not to trap you into a life of decadence!

She watched his hard, lean body covertly from beneath the dark sweep of her lashes and thought, most uncharacteristically, that perhaps in *this* case decadence might have something to commend it!

'Did you have a coat?' he asked as he pushed open one of the glass doors to receive the cold night air.

'N-no.' Her teeth had begun to chatter. When she had left the house earlier it had been a deceptively warm and starry evening, but now a breeze was fluttering its cool fingers through the air.

'Here, then—you're cold,' he said, frowning, and immediately removed his jacket to hang it loosely over her shoulders.

He turned left out of the tennis club towards East Road, as though he instinctively knew the way, and Lola wrinkled her nose. 'But this is the way to my house,' she said.

'Don't sound so surprised. Wasn't the general idea to head in the direction of your house—as that's where I'm supposed to be taking you?'

'But I don't remember telling you where I lived.'

'You must have done,' he answered quickly. 'Or how could I have known?'

How indeed? Lola hugged his jacket closer, obsessively observing her surroundings in an effort not to concentrate on the tantalisingly subtle scents of musk and lemon which clung to his coat, but it wasn't easy.

Huge banks of dark, glossy laurels lined the road, looming high on either side, protecting the vast houses behind them from the curious eyes of onlookers. Occasionally, there were high, impenetrable gates, bearing a stark picture of a barking guard dog that was meant to deter burglars—or curious sightseers, desperate to catch a glimpse of some of the houses and their often famous occupants.

In fact, Lola had long since decided that the word 'house' was a bit of a misnomer where St Fiacre's was concerned. The smallest residence on the estate had six bedrooms, and the largest was rumoured to have twenty-two!

It was the world of the hidden camera and the stony-faced guard which so often went hand in hand with money—although the lush green acres surrounding the houses did much to compensate for the downside of extreme wealth.

She and Geraint walked side by side. Twice, cars slowed down—large, opulent and expensive cars, whose drivers were interested to know why a couple were actually *walking* around St Fiacre's instead of driving!

Lola often thought that most of her neighbours wouldn't know what to do with their hands if they weren't holding a steering wheel!

They had almost reached the dip in the road where a branch of East Road ran up to join North Road when Lola said, pointing into a curving driveway, 'I live here.'

He glanced up the drive to where the elegant white three-storey building sat amidst carefully manicured lawns. But instead of commenting on the house Geraint paused to look at Lola instead, his hard-boned face a series of shifting shadows cast by the pale moon and the even paler light from the stars.

'You do realise that we've met before?' he said suddenly.

Lola found that she couldn't stop herself from smiling, ridiculously pleased that he *had* remembered. Of course, bearing in mind his no doubt colossal ego, she really ought to feign ignorance of *him*, but she dismissed the idea immediately. She wasn't a good liar at the best of times and for some reason she baulked at the thought of Geraint finding her out in a lie!

She nodded, her glossy hair full of moonlight. 'Yes, I do. It was on a flight out of London to Paris, wasn't it?'

'Ah! So you *do* remember.'

'Yes,' agreed Lola calmly.

'But you didn't mention it.'

Lola fixed him with a direct look. 'Neither did you.'

'Maybe I thought that you wouldn't remember a mere passenger—you must see thousands of men every working week.'

'Not remember *you*?' Lola gave a pale imitation of a smile. 'Oh, come on, Mr Howell-Williams— please don't indulge in false modesty on my account! You happen to be a very memorable man, as I'm sure countless women have told you. I remember you very well, as it happens. You kept requesting tomato juice.'

'Heavens!' he mocked. 'You really do have a good memory, don't you?' He lifted his dark brows questioningly. 'So why did you keep glaring at me whenever I asked you for another drink?'

Lola shifted in embarrassment. 'It doesn't matter.'

'Oh, but it does.' In the darkness his grey eyes were as cold and as glittering as the finest marble and Lola recognised that he was the kind of man who would chip away until he'd obtained all the answers he wanted.

She decided to give in without a struggle. 'If you must know, I suspected your motives.'

He stilled. 'My motives?' he asked, in an odd, quiet sort of voice. 'Just what do you mean by that?'

Lola shook her head. 'Really—it isn't important.'

'Oh, but it is,' he contradicted her, in a voice suddenly soft with menace. 'Tell me.'

Lola gave him a steady look, realising that the atmosphere between them had suddenly changed to a big freeze, and wondering why.

She shrugged. 'OK. I'll tell you if you insist. We keep the tomato juice on the bottom shelf of the trolley because it is one of our least popular drinks. Some of the male passengers seem to have cottoned on to this, and they keep asking for it so that...that...' Her voice trailed off in embarrassment as she saw the contempt hardening his lips. Oh, *why* hadn't she kept her big mouth shut?

'So that you have to bend right down to get it?' he finished for her acidly.

Lola blushed again. Hateful, *perceptive* man! 'Well, yes,' she admitted, the look on his face making her wish that a hole could open up in front of her and swallow her up.

'Do you really think,' he said witheringly, 'that I would be reduced to resorting to such juvenile ploys? And if I *did* want to see your knickers I would hardly need to make myself sick through drinking excessive amounts of tomato juice. After all, those abbreviated outfits that you wear for work leave very little to the imagination!'

'Why, you—' Maddened beyond thinking, Lola swung her hand out to slap his face, but his reactions were much too speedy for her, and he caught her wrist easily, pulling her right up against his chest and looking down at her, his wolfish smile making his shadowed face look both intimidating and delectably kissable.

'You what?' he mocked. 'Beast? Brute? Bastard? Some or all of those? Want to think badly of me, do you, Lola Hennessy? Well, why not have something to *really* focus your anger on?'

And he did what she had been wanting him to do all evening. He gathered her into his arms and crushed his mouth down on hers in a kiss which sent all her senses into overdrive.

She was aware of the sweetness, of the intimacy as their tongues locked, of the desperate need to hold onto him as tightly as possible and never let him go.

She heard the low moan he made in the back of his throat as he sought to pull her even closer against him and Lola clung onto those wide, strong shoulders, massaging them like a woman possessed, the rocky bulge of his muscles steel-hard against her fingertips.

She could feel the leanness of his abdomen against her rounded belly, and she could sense the tension in him as he shifted his weight, moving his hips in a distracted circle, which made her acutely aware of just how easily he could be turned on too.

The realisation that things were spiralling out of control was what cleared Lola's mind from the constricting mists of desire, and the facts began to seep coldly into her brain as she forced herself to remember how he had insulted her.

And yet here she was allowing herself to be meekly compromised by necking in a bush with him!

Angrily, she pushed him away. 'I don't know what you think you're—'

'Oh, spare me the hysterics, do,' he interrupted calmly, and then he actually *yawned*—although Lola was convinced that it was deliberate! 'When will you women realise that it really doesn't count if you declare your unwillingness *after* the event? Particularly,' he drawled insultingly, 'when your willingness to participate was overwhelming at the time.'

His grey eyes glinted with remembered pleasure. 'That was some kiss,' he murmured softly, his eyes narrowing as he looked down at her, seeming taken aback by the dazed look on her face. And some of the abrasiveness had left his voice when he said, 'Come on—I'll walk you to the door.'

For about ten seconds Lola was completely speechless and then she made up for it. 'Do you really think that I would let you anywhere *near* my house after that?' she spluttered indignantly.

'Why ever not?' He looked perplexed.

'Because I'm not used to being man-handled by jumped-up Lotharios who think that caveman tactics will have a woman swooning in their arms every time!'

'And you are claiming *not* to have enjoyed my so-called caveman tactics?' he drawled, his eyes glittering as he recalled that Lola had done exactly that. 'I rest my case,' he added insultingly as her hot, guilty cheeks added fuel to his argument.

'Perhaps you'd better go,' she suggested from between gritted teeth. Before she said something she might regret, she added silently.

'Go? Sure.' He gave her an unsettling smile and turned away with a lazy assurance which filled Lola with an inexplicable kind of fear. He did not look like a man who was going too far.

'Goodnight, Lola.'

'Wh-where are you going?'

'Home.' He raised his dark brows at her in sultry question. 'Unless that was an oblique invitation for me to stay?'

'Wh-where do you live?' she demanded nervously. 'On the estate?'

He smiled. 'I'm afraid so. Although only temporarily, you understand. I'm staying at Dominic Dashwood's house.'

'B-but that's next door!' Lola spluttered. 'To *me*!'

'Exactly. So we'll be neighbours.' His eyes glinted with a wickedness that excited her, and with something else, too—something which unsettled her, unnerved her. Something she couldn't define.

A chill, nebulous dread settled on her skin like a fog as she tried to imagine Geraint Howell-Williams living next door.

'N-neighbours?' she stumbled.

'Mmm. Now won't that be fun, Lola?'

CHAPTER TWO

THE trolley rattled like a brass band as Lola struggled to push it up the last few yards of the aisle with something approaching dignity.

Perhaps Geraint Howell-Williams was right, she reflected as she tugged the tiny skirt down over her bottom. The yellow minis, edged with blue piping, left very little to the imagination. Or was it just something to do with her own rather curvy figure, which made the already inadequate skirt seem to ride even higher up her thighs?

And what the hell are you doing even *thinking* about Geraint Howell-Williams, anyway? she asked herself crossly. He is just a man you met for about an *hour* last night. A rude, arrogant, egotistical man who kissed you without asking permission first and let things rapidly get out of control. That's how much you mean to him. That's how much he respects you.

And you *hate* him! she told herself fiercely.

The only trouble was that saying the same thing over and over again did not necessarily make you believe it. She had already spent an almost sleepless night alternatively fretting and fuming, punching the pillow with a violence which alarmed her, and then feverishly burying her head in it as if it were Geraint's face, like a woman possessed.

Consequently, she had drifted off just before the alarm clock rang, and she had staggered out of bed feeling like death—dreading the thought of having to face a flight to Rome, and then a stopover there.

By the time Lola pushed the trolley into the gallery, her best friend Marnie was waiting for her, pinching olives from the left-over hors d'oeuvres and shoving them into her mouth like a hamster.

Lola loved flying, but it was even better when you were working with someone you knew. And she and Marnie had started working at Atalanta Airlines together on the very same day, almost seven years ago.

'You look terrible,' observed Marnie, offering Lola an olive.

Lola waved her hand in refusal. 'Thanks very much,' she said waspishly.

'Didn't you sleep?'

Lola sighed. 'You could say that.'

'Any particular reason?'

Lola shook her head. It would not do her already pitiful reputation with men any good if she admitted to losing sleep over someone who was little more than a passing acquaintance!

'Never mind.' Marnie thoughtfully removed a piece of pimento from her fingernail. 'I know just the thing to cheer you up. Or rather just the man! Have you noticed him yet?'

Lola began unloading the trays and wrinkled her nose. How she wished that people would not stub their cigarettes out in the sherry trifle! 'Who?' she asked absently. 'Don't tell me the captain has emerged from the cockpit and is strolling about smiling graciously and being pleasant to all the passengers?'

'No, no, *no*!' said Marnie. 'Nothing as far-fetched as that! No, I mean the guy two rows from the front in First Class.'

'But I'm not *working* in First Class,' Lola pointed out patiently. 'Am I?'

'That hasn't stopped every other stewardess on the flight making it their business to go and look at him. Or should I say *ogle* him?'

'I never look at passengers in that way,' said Lola haughtily. 'It's unprofessional!'

Marnie had now started picking prawns off tiny triangles of brown bread and was curling them into her mouth with a long scarlet talon. 'No, you don't look at passengers—but you somehow get one of them to leave you a whacking great mansion worth almost a million pounds! Nice work, Lola!'

Lola opened her mouth to protest, as she seemed to have been protesting ever since the totally un-expected legacy had come her way, then shut it again. She had all but given up trying to explain away her unexpected stroke of fortune.

Even if she painted the facts as baldly as possible—that a passenger she had met through her job and her charity work with the airline had taken a shine to her and left her a whacking great house—well, people still put two and two together and came out with a rather grubby five.

Sex, sex, sex. That was all anybody seemed to think about these days! And even if the giver of the house had been over sixty and the recipient a mere twenty-five all but the very nicest people tended to think that Lola had had a red-hot affair with him.

When the truth was that she had never had a red-hot affair with *anyone*!

'How's your mother?' asked Marnie. 'Has she seen the mighty inheritance yet?'

Lola shook her head, so that the jaunty blue and yellow cap which all the cabin crew absolutely *loathed* looked in danger of toppling from her high-piled curls. 'Nope,' she answered gloomily. 'Doesn't want to know anything about it. I've tried telling her that everything associated with the wretched house is above board, but I don't think she believes me.'

'Oh, she'll come around,' said Marnie comfortingly. 'And it isn't as though she was always visiting you when you lived in the flat, is it?'

'No,' answered Lola reflectively. 'She's a very solitary sort of person, I guess. Doesn't mix much.'

'Unlike you,' smiled Marnie.

Lola shrugged. 'I don't seem to have been mixing much recently—the house takes up every bit of my spare time, it's so big!'

'My heart *bleeds* for you!' mocked Marnie.

'Then come and live there too!' offered Lola impulsively. 'There's plenty of room.'

Marnie shook her head. She was engaged to be married and she didn't want to share Rob with anyone, not even Lola. 'Just because you want a tame member of staff?' she quizzed jokingly. 'No way!'

Lola looked down to find that someone had smeared most of a vegetarian rissole all over the side of their tray. She tutted. Passengers could be absolutely infuriating sometimes.

'Lola?'

Lola turned around at the gentle tap on her shoulder.

It was Stuart, the purser, the flight attendant in charge of all the cabin crew. 'I'd like one of you two girls to come up and help out in First Class, please,' he said. 'We're run off our feet up there.'

Marnie winked meaningfully at Lola. 'With pleasure,' she purred. 'I'll be right along, Stuart.'

The purser shook his head. 'I'll take Lola, if you don't mind, Marnie. She's the only female on board who seems to have any common sense to speak of.'

'Why, thank you, Stuart!' Lola beamed. 'Recognition at long last! Does that mean promotion is about to wing its way to me?'

'It means,' growled Stuart, 'that you seem to be the only woman on board this flight who hasn't fluttered up to that man in First Class on some pathetic pretext or other, that was so patently transparent he must have been laughing all over his face. I really don't know what they all see in him!'

'You just wait!' mouthed Marnie to Lola.

'He's bound to have an ego the size of Wembley Stadium!' commented Lola, pulling a face. 'I had an awful night, Stuart, with hardly any sleep to speak of—must I really go and pander to some pretty little rich boy with an over-inflated sense of his own importance?'

Stuart laughed. 'Go on with you! I want someone up there who won't come over all silly when she sets eyes on him! Just go and tidy yourself up a bit first, would you, Lola?'

'Cheek!' Lola retorted, but she checked her hair and slicked on a bit of lipstick and scraped a particularly stubborn curl back into her tortoiseshell

hair-clip, before making her way to First Class, her
eyes automatically straying to two rows from the
front on the right-hand side, where Marnie had said
that . . . that . . .

Lola broke out into a cold sweat, shaking her
head in a desperate kind of denial. She took a deep
breath, shut her eyes very briefly, then looked again.

It was him.

Definitely him.

Geraint Howell-Williams was on *her* flight, and
if she didn't get out of the way very quickly he
would see her, and she would have to serve him,
and—

'Excuse me, *stewardess*,' came a deep, mocking
voice, and Lola saw, to her absolute horror, that
the dark head had turned around and that she was
very firmly fixed in the gaze of a pair of stormy
grey eyes.

For one mad moment she thought of pretending
that she had not heard him, of turning tail and
running back up to the other end of the aeroplane,
but of course she couldn't do that. She had a fan-
tastic work record at Atalanta Airlines and she was
damned if she was going to let Geraint Howell-
Williams interfere with that!

Unconsciously smoothing down her skirt, she
glided over to him in her most professional manner,
and gave him a frosty smile which she hoped no
one but him would recognise as being supercilious.

'Yes, sir? What can I get you?'

'You could try getting rid of that superior expression on your face,' he answered softly.

She kept the saccharine smile fixed firmly to her lips. 'If I look superior, sir, then perhaps it's because I *am* superior.'

He stared up at her innocently. 'Are you trying to offend me, Lola?'

'Yes.'

'I thought so.'

A suspicion leapt to the forefront of her mind.

Geraint Howell-Williams had now travelled with Atalanta Airlines twice in the past few weeks and before that she had never noticed him. And she would definitely have noticed him. 'Are you following me?' she quizzed.

There was an infinitesimal pause. A briefly guarded look hardened the devastating face before the grey eyes cleared and looked up at her with studied amusement. 'Is that an occupational hazard, then, being followed? Perhaps it happens to you a lot, Lola?' he suggested sardonically.

'Oh, ha, ha, ha!' she retorted crossly.

'And I have to say that much as I admire your riotous curls and bright blue eyes and luscious curves—' his eyes glinted '—do you really think I'd go to all the trouble of taking flights around all the major capital cities in Europe just so that I could catch a glimpse of them?'

When he put it like that, her question sounded absolutely ludicrous. 'I suppose not,' she answered, and forced herself to wait for his order without squirming.

It was strange, really, that in all her years of flying she had never had a problem about being in a servile position with passengers. Until *now*.

For the first time ever she found herself resenting having to stand with a polite smile glued to her mouth, when, if the truth be known, she would have liked to stomp off down the aircraft and as far away from Geraint Howell-Williams as possible!

He stretched his legs out lazily in front of him, and Lola's eyes were reluctantly drawn to the muscular shafts of his thighs.

Reclining, he seemed even taller, if that were possible. The seats in First Class were specifically designed to give the passengers more leg-room—but, even so, Geraint's legs only *just* fitted comfortably.

An incomprehensible light lit the stormy grey eyes as he glanced up to find her gaze riveted to the lower half of his body. 'Does looking at my legs give you pleasure, Lola?'

That was just the trouble—it *did*! She had been having all kinds of impure thoughts about them, and the most disturbing thing was that she was discovering that with Mr Geraint Howell-Williams she could very definitely respond to him on two levels.

On a social level she would have liked to march him down the aircraft and boot him into the hold with all the suitcases—as a kind of punishment for his outrageous cheek and determination to embarrass her. Whereas on a physical level . . .

She somehow managed to keep her blush at bay and gave him a calm, empty sort of look. 'I haven't really given them a lot of thought, to be honest, *sir*.'

'No?' he queried softly.

'No,' she answered repressively.

'Liar!' he taunted.

'*Mr* Howell-Williams—'

'Oh, Geraint, please; we're a little too—um—*familiar* to stand on ceremony, wouldn't you say?'

She carried on speaking as if he had not interrupted her with that timely little reminder of how she had swooned in his arms last night. 'I am not paid to be insulted by passengers, no matter what section of the aircraft they are sitting in. Do you understand?'

'Yes, miss,' he answered meekly.

Lola glared, but it took an effort. A huge effort. How extraordinarily annoying it was that she wanted to just curl up at his feet and melt with pleasure at that little-boy-lost look he was subjecting her to at the moment.

'What would you like?' she asked, indicating the drinks list in front of him. 'Champagne?'

'Not particularly.' He shrugged. 'Champagne is essentially a drink of celebration and there isn't really a lot to celebrate with me sitting down here and you standing there, dressed in that ridiculous uniform—'

'It is *not* a ridiculous uniform! It's just...'

As if controlled by an outside force, their eyes were simultaneously drawn to the saffron-coloured jacket and matching short, short skirt she wore, all piped in a rather hideous shade of cornflower-blue.

Never in her life had Lola been quite so aware of the amount of thigh on view—and rather chubby thigh, come to that, because she certainly wasn't built on the same scale as some of the skeletal beauties who worked alongside her.

'A little on the short side?' he supplied helpfully, and his gaze roved with undisguised interest up the entire length of her legs. 'Though I have to say that from where I'm sitting...'

'You sexist pig!'

He shrugged. 'What's sexist about admiring your legs? You were admiring mine—'

'I was *not*!' declared Lola heatedly.

'Is anything the matter, sir?'

Stuart had glided silently up to Geraint's seat and he shot Lola a questioning look as her heart sank.

Wait for it, she thought. He's going to say goodness only knows what about me, and I won't have a leg to stand on! The passenger in front must have heard me calling Geraint a sexist pig, and we are taught never, never, *never*—no matter what the provocation—to insult the passenger!

She sighed resignedly as she saw Geraint open his mouth to speak and blanked from her mind the inevitable scene as she imagined him relating her rudeness to the purser.

Thank heavens for my inheritance, she thought, with a fleeting flash of humour. At least I'll be able to sell the house and live off the interest until I decide what I want to do with the rest of my life...

'How lovely!' Stuart was beaming at her, his face wreathed with unfamiliar smiles.

'L-lovely?' stumbled Lola in confusion. 'What's lovely?'

'That you're having dinner with Mr Howell-Williams tonight.'

Lola narrowed her eyes and was challenged by a spectacular grey gaze. '*I* am having *dinner* with Mr Howell-Williams?' she repeated incredulously. '*Tonight?*'

Stuart looked slightly bewildered. 'Well, that's what he said—'

'Oh, Lola likes to play hard to get,' came a voice of silky amusement with an underlying hint of steel. 'Don't you, sweetheart?'

Stuart nearly dropped his bottle of Cabernet Sauvignon at the easy familiarity conjured up by the word 'sweetheart'. 'So you two *know* each other?' he quizzed eagerly.

'We're neighbours,' Geraint revealed.

'*Oh.*' Stuart seemed fascinated by this. 'You live at St Fiacre's too, do you?'

Geraint smiled. 'Only for the time being, until I find a place I like enough to want to buy. I'm renting my friend Dominic Dashwood's house—he's gone away for the winter.'

Barbados, probably, thought Lola, or somewhere equally exotic. Dominic Dashwood was the neighbour she hardly ever saw, and he made other rich men look like paupers. His wealth was legendary—but not nearly as legendary as his reputation and appetite for beautiful women.

Stuart beamed at Lola. 'You should have *said* that you knew each other! Mind you,' he confided to Geraint, 'our Lola always gets on exceptionally well with the passengers! Gets more invitations to dinner than anyone else on the craft—*and* the occasional surprise present from a passenger!' He winked at Lola, and moved away down the aisle.

'Oh, does she?' asked Geraint tonelessly, scarcely seeming to notice that Stuart had left, and for a moment Lola was aware of an odd look in his narrowed grey eyes. A fierce, intent kind of look. Just for a moment there Geraint Howell-Williams had looked almost...almost...*bitter*...

'There's no rule against accepting gifts from passengers!' Lola stated, extremely irritated by that critical look on his face, which made her sound much more flippant than she usually did. And which, she realised, had the unfortunate effect of making herself sound like some kind of second-rate gold-digger!

The flippancy made him wince, and Lola was aware of an unsettling feeling of disquiet stealing over her, as if his disapproval of her somehow diminished her in her *own* eyes.

'And that's your main criterion for living, is it?' he questioned quietly. 'That if there is no rule against it then it must be OK?'

'Please don't put words into my mouth,' returned Lola softly.

He studied her face for a moment before speaking. 'I don't intend to. I intend to put food into your mouth instead. What time shall I pick you up tonight?'

But Lola shook her head, hoping that her reluctance to do what she knew to be the right thing did not show. 'I don't think that's such a good idea, do you?'

His mouth thinned into something resembling a smile. 'Why else would I suggest it?'

Lola looked up and down the cabin quickly, to check that none of the other staff were in earshot, and then she lowered her voice. 'Look—perhaps I gave you the wrong idea last night—'

'That would depend on your definition of "wrong", surely, Lola?' he demurred softly. 'I certainly had no problem with your behaviour last night—'

'I'll *bet* you didn't!' Lola snapped, her cheeks growing hot as she remembered her virtual surrender in his arms. 'And if I hadn't stopped it who *knows* where we would have ended up?'

'I hardly think you need the brains of Einstein to work that one out for yourself,' he responded drily.

Lola felt her fingers itching frantically and in that moment longed to slap him.

It was extraordinary. She had tried to slap him last night, too—that had been how the kiss had started. She, normally the most peaceable of people, had started exhibiting the most uncharacteristic behaviour!

Just why did she react so violently and so uniquely to this one particular man? Would an analyst say that the violence was a substitute for sex—because subconsciously she desired him, even though there was something about him which made her wonder whether she could trust him?

She took a deep breath and hoped that she was managing to present a calm, neutral face. 'The aircraft is full, and I'm very busy. So would you please excuse me now, Mr Howell-Williams—unless you've decided what you want me to get you?'

'Tomato juice, please,' he said, deadpan, and Lola pursed her lips.

'Are you trying to be funny?'

'Well, I was, yes,' he admitted, and gave her a heart-stopping grin.

And it was that grin which proved her absolute undoing. She actually began to dimple back at him—her face soon lit up by a huge, helpless smile. 'I'd better go and get your drink—'

He stayed her with nothing more than a look—cool and provocative and very, very assured. Lola would have defied *anyone* to resist a look like that.

'I don't want a drink,' he said quietly. 'I just want you to agree to have dinner with me tonight.'

Lola felt goose-bumps jump up all over her skin. She had a powerful premonition of just how vulnerable she might be to this man's exceptional allure. That was, if she let herself... She opened her mouth to refuse, but Geraint pre-empted her.

'And what if I tell the purser you were being outrageously rude to me just now?' he mused. 'And accused me of being a sexist pig. And that now you're refusing to allow me the opportunity to clear my name?'

'That's called blackmail,' protested Lola, but only half-heartedly.

'That's called getting your own way,' he corrected her.

'Which I suppose you always do?'

He gave an unrepentant smile. 'What do you think?'

'I think it's about time someone turned you down,' she told him fiercely.

'For my own good?' he mocked.

Lola shrugged. 'Perhaps.'

'And you think you could be that person?'

She gave him a level look, her sky-blue eyes dazzling him. 'Why not?'

'Because I'm not going to take no for an answer, that's why. Not from you. So what have you got to say about that, Lola Hennessy?'

It was a pointless question when accompanied by a glittering look of approbation which would have made the most committed man-hater melt into submission! It was like asking a prisoner if they would like to taste freedom again!

Lola found Geraint Howell-Williams outrageously attractive, yes, but highly disturbing too. She sensed that sexually he was light years ahead of her, but the reason for her disquiet went deeper than that.

For there was an almost tangible air of danger about him, a danger which surrounded him like an aura and yet only added to his buccaneer-like appeal. She could almost imagine him in a billowing white shirt, a gleaming sword held aloft as he fought off invaders!

She swallowed the image down; it was inexplicably making her want to kiss him again.

'Lola?' he prompted, his voice a throaty caress. 'Are you going to have dinner with me tonight?'

'Yes, I am,' she told him without hesitation, because at that precise moment—rightly or wrongly—it was what she wanted more than anything else in the world.

CHAPTER THREE

'SO WHAT are you going to *wear* for this date of the century?' Marnie yelled.

Lola made an ugly face at herself in the mirror. 'That's the trouble—I don't *know*!' She pulled the belt of her towelling robe even tighter and walked out of the bathroom into the rather luxurious room which Atalanta Airlines had assigned to her. Situated slap bang in the middle of the city centre, the New Rome Hotel commanded a magnificent view over the ancient capital.

Lola and Marnie had checked in just over an hour ago, and now Marnie was sitting on Lola's bed, drinking a very large gin and tonic and ploughing through the bowl of courtesy nuts with the dedicated air of an animal preparing for hibernation.

She looked up as Lola strolled into the bedroom, and winced. 'Haven't you overdone the scent a bit?'

Lola, who had used enough bath oil to fill the hotel swimming pool, wrinkled her nose. 'Oh, it'll fade,' she said confidently.

Marnie shook her head as Lola began to rub vigorously at her hair with a towel. 'And I can't *believe* you washed your hair. You know how thick it is—you'll *never* get it dry in time!'

'Gee, thanks! You're supposed to be here to encourage me, not to add to my nerves!' said Lola. She pulled on a pair of white cotton knickers, turning to look in another mirror and automatically sucking her stomach in as she did so. *Still* podgy, she thought in despair. 'Should I wear my scarlet dress, do you think? Or the black? Which makes me look thinner?'

Marnie raised her eyes heavenwards. 'Do you want to fall into bed with him in the first ten minutes?'

'Of course I don't!'

Marnie shrugged. 'There's no need to look so outraged.'

'Oh, isn't there?' Lola glared at her friend indignantly. 'Do you think I always hop into bed with men on the first date?'

Marnie smiled. 'Of course I don't! But then you don't go out on dates with men who look like Geraint Howell-Williams very often.'

'And what's so special about Geraint Howell-Williams?' demanded Lola hotly. 'He just happens to be richer and better-looking than most men, that's all.'

'No!' Marnie shook her head with all the wisdom of her two years' seniority over Lola. 'That's not all. It's much more than that—and you've got to be careful, Lola!'

'Careful?'

Marnie nodded. 'How can I put it? I know! If all men are tadpoles—'

'I *like* the comparison!' quipped Lola immediately.

Marnie silenced her with a look. 'Then Geraint Howell-Williams is the killer shark!' she finished dramatically. 'Dangerous. Experienced. Downright gorgeous. Irresistible. Do you see what I mean, Lola?'

'I wasn't aware that sharks were gorgeous and irresistible,' joked Lola. 'Perhaps I should take up marine science!'

'Stop it—I'm serious! I don't trust him! He's too hunky for his own good!'

'I asked for advice on my choice of gown, not a character assassination of my escort,' answered Lola airily.

'All right—I'll give you my advice! Don't wear the black *or* the scarlet—'

'But—'

'Wear nothing but sackcloth—and if you don't have sackcloth then reach for the dullest, most uninspiring outfit in your suitcase. Whatever you would choose to wear to tea with your most shockable maiden aunt, add an all-enveloping cardigan to it! Put on thick stockings and flat shoes for good measure. Oh, and don't wear any make-up! That way Geraint Howell-Williams will not look at you with lust in his eyes, and you will not be tempted into gaining carnal knowledge of him!'

'Thanks for nothing!' groaned Lola as she flicked through the contents of her wardrobe. 'I don't want to look as though I'm trying too hard—but then again I *do* want to look my best. A woman has her pride to think about,' she defended herself staunchly as she saw Marnie's eyes narrow suspiciously.

In the end, she simply wore her hair loose to give it a chance to dry properly, and chose a trouser suit in butter-cream silk, with wide pyjama-style trousers which fastened tightly at her ankles, and a jacket fashioned like a frock-coat.

Like most of her silk clothes, she had had it made up for her on a trip to Hong Kong, but she had only worn it once before, for the simple reason that it attracted dirt like a seven-year-old schoolboy!

She did a twirl in the centre of the room. 'What do you think?'

Marnie was uncharacteristically silent for a moment. Then she said, 'You look stunning, Lola,' and added in a worried voice, 'You *will* be careful, won't you?'

'Of course I'll be careful! Stop sounding as though we're bit-players in a spy movie!'

'Where's he taking you?'

Lola tried and failed to keep the glee out of her voice. 'The Mimosa.'

Marnie scowled. 'I don't want to be impressed— but I am! You lucky, lucky thing—I've always wanted to eat there but it costs more than a year's salary! And Rob says that even if he was loaded he wouldn't spend that kind of money on a meal, on principle. What time is he collecting you?'

Lola glanced down at the watch which gleamed discreetly on her wrist. 'Oh, my goodness!' she squeaked. 'Right now!'

Marnie held her hand up authoritatively. 'Then let him wait! It would do a man like that good to be kept waiting!' she added darkly.

So Lola made herself wait for five minutes which seemed to tick away like five hours before she set off downstairs to find him. He was easily located in the hotel lobby and her eyes were drawn instantly to his dark, elegant body.

He was lounging in one of the squashy leather sofas with his long legs stretched out in front of him, his head resting back on his hands so that those narrowed slate-grey eyes missed nothing.

He saw her immediately and stood up with a kind of unconscious animal grace which had more than one female head swivelling eagerly in his direction.

He was wearing an unstructured suit in a wonderful shade of pale grey, and the loose-fitting cut of the jacket and trousers was somehow the sexiest thing that Lola had ever seen.

Geraint's appeal was all subtlety and understatement, she realised, as opposed to the glaringly obvious. She could certainly never imagine him in skin-tight jeans. Well, on second thoughts perhaps she could! Only too well...

His expression was difficult to define as he followed her movements through the foyer, but he was frowning slightly, as though something about her puzzled him. But when Lola gave him a questioning look the watchfulness was replaced by a bland, social smile of greeting.

'You look quite—exotic,' he commented slowly.

'D-do I?' Even as she was speaking the words, Lola was shuddering inwardly at how absolutely wet she sounded. And hadn't he sounded rather doubtful about her outfit? Had *exotic* been the effect she had been searching for?

He ran a finger slowly over one silken buttercream cuff and just that one innocuous little touch made Lola shiver like a cat that had been left out in the rain all night.

'I had it made in Hong Kong,' she added rather breathlessly, more to fill in the rather awkward silence which had fallen than because she seriously thought he might be interested in her dressmaking tips!

He gave a lazy smile. 'Really?'

Lola swallowed. Was he going to persist in making her feel uncomfortable all evening with his sardonic comments? More importantly, was she going to let him?

'Why did you ask me to have dinner with you tonight, Geraint?' she demanded.

'Let's discuss it in the taxi, shall we?' he said, putting his hand firmly underneath her elbow and guiding her out of the door—with Lola acutely and embarrassingly aware of all the incredulous looks she was getting from the other women.

He must have felt her stiffen as the plate-glass doors closed behind them, for he looked down at her. 'What is it?' he demanded quietly. 'What's the matter?'

Lola tried to make a joke of it—for he must have noticed the reactions of the people in the foyer, too—but she knew that her voice only ended up sounding wistful. 'All those beautiful women in there—they're wondering what on earth you're doing with someone who looks like me!'

He gave her a thoughtful glance as he opened the door of the taxi which had materialised as if by magic, and helped her inside.

'Beautiful?' he echoed wryly, then shook his dark head. 'I don't find stick-like bodies coupled with all-revealing clothes in the least bit beautiful. Whereas that silk suit you're wearing...'

His eyes roved almost reluctantly over her, observing how the butter-cream silk clung faintly to every undulation of her body. 'It hints rather than broadcasts, tantalises rather than emblazons,' he murmured. 'I find that infinitely more attractive than the kind of dress which threatens the wearer with being hauled up on an indecency charge.'

'Oh,' said Lola rather indistinctly, feeling ridiculously cheered by his obvious approval.

She was then rather nonplussed to see him lean forward and start speaking to the driver in rapid Italian. 'You're fluent!' she observed in surprise.

He gave a half-smile. 'You find that so remarkable?'

'Yes, I do. Most Englishmen—'

'Ah! But I'm not English, Lola—I'm Welsh.'

'Oh, I see.' So *that* explained the faint, almost musical lilt which made the deep voice so distinctive. And the tar-black tousled hair—its wildness only contained by the superb way he had had it cut.

She shot a covert glance at his impressive frame, at the broad shoulders and the rock-hard muscle of his thighs, visualising him on a ploughed-up field, blocking the other players' every attempt to pass him. 'And d-did you play rugby?' she managed as she made a feeble attempt to squash the lustful vision of Geraint in a pair of mud-spattered shorts.

'So you're stereotyping me now, are you?' he mocked her softly. 'The man is Welsh, therefore he must play rugby and sing in an all-male choir! Right?'

'No! I'm not stereotyping you!' she protested, but she saw the hint of dark humour in his eyes and shrugged helplessly. 'I'm only trying to be pleasant!'

'Pleasant is fine,' he teased. 'But a little dull, surely, Lola?'

Lola sighed. If only he didn't have the ability to make her tremble just by the seductive way he pronounced her name! 'I don't see how we can have a halfway decent evening if you block my every attempt at conversation with some smart remark like that!' she objected.

'You don't *have* to make conversation with me, you know, sweetheart,' he told her with an air of lazy containment.

'Really?' she enquired archly. 'Then what else do you propose I do? And please don't come out with something crass and obvious!'

He gave a low laugh. 'I have no intention of being either of those.'

'Good.' She looked at him questioningly, her heart thumping very loudly in her ears.

He smiled. 'Well, I rather like the way you look at me, when you're trying your best not to. So why don't you carry on gazing at me adoringly for now and we can save the life-stories for during dinner?'

Lola was outraged. What arrogance! Carry on gazing at him, indeed! And *adoringly*, too! *Had* she been? Oh, if only she had the strength of character to force him to turn the cab round and take her straight back to the hotel where she could spend the evening with Marnie.

Except that by now Marnie would have decamped with the rest of the crew to one of Rome's noisiest discos and Lola would either have to eat a solitary meal in the hotel dining room or have something delivered up to her room.

And she didn't want to. She *wanted* to be here. And with him. That was the trouble.

Surreptitiously sliding along the seat as far away from him as possible, Lola stared fixedly out of the window at the passing city with the sinking realisation that it didn't seem to matter what kind of outrageous statements he came out with. Or how much he put her back up. Because she wanted him with all the fierce intensity of a woman who had just discovered desire for the first time in her life.

And because it hadn't happened until she had reached the comparatively ripe old age of twenty-five it seemed to have hit her with the most overwhelming force.

She found herself at the mercy of new and rather frightening feelings, found that she wanted to do all those things she had previously thought were the province of the emotionally unstable—to tremble, and to weep, to reach out and touch him...

And didn't all those things sound suspiciously like the symptoms of love?

She gave her head a tiny shake of denial—you simply did *not* fall in love with people you hardly knew!

'Stop sulking,' he urged softly.

'I am *not* sulking. I'm enjoying the view.'

The Mimosa was easily recognisable with its hundreds of tiny white lights threaded into the still bare branches of the trees outside. Lola spotted people queuing around the block in an attempt to secure a table.

'We're here!' she exclaimed, inadvertently tugging the sleeve of Geraint's jacket in her excitement. 'And just look at all the fairy lights—it's absolutely beautiful!'

Her enthusiasm produced a look from Geraint which was half-indulgent and half-perplexed, as if he wasn't used to such exuberant behaviour. But he said nothing before they were led through the restaurant and seated at what was, quite simply, the best table in the room.

'So how did you manage to swing this?' Lola asked as she broke a bread stick in half and crunched on it.

'What? A date with you?'

'The table,' she told him.

'Oh, that bit wasn't difficult. Certainly not as difficult as securing the date.'

'No?' She studied him in disbelief. 'That's why all those people outside are virtually trying to break the door down to get in, is it?'

He shrugged. 'I speak Italian. I do a lot of business here. I adore the country—the food, the wine and the culture. Given all those things, finding a table in a good restaurant doesn't pose much of a problem.'

He made it sound as easy as ABC! Lola finished chomping on her bread stick and picked up another, to find him looking at her with reluctant approval. He obviously *did* like women who enjoyed their food, she thought in amazement, but that did not mean that she had to go over the top and completely pig out!

She put the bread stick carefully back down in front of her. 'I don't want to spoil my appetite,' she explained.

'Maybe we'd better order?' he suggested with a smile, and he must have elevated an eyebrow or

moved a broad shoulder or *something*, Lola decided, since the waiter appeared as if on cue.

The next couple of minutes were spent discussing
the wine list and the recommended dishes and Lola
tried to appear interested in her choices, but she
might as well have ordered bread and sawdust—for
the normal pleasure she took in anticipating her
meal had been totally eclipsed by Geraint's
presence.

She felt as gauche as a teenager out on a first
date, which was absolutely ridiculous! She had enjoyed lots of dates, *and* what she had thought was
going to be a fairly heavy love-affair with a pilot,
not long after she had started at Atalanta Airlines.
But she had been far too young to cope with a
smooth operator who seemed to be out of the
country more often than he was in it.

The memory of that relationship still had the
power to make her ask herself incredulously how
she could have been such a *fool*.

The affair had ended before it had even begun—
very painfully—with Lola's shocked discovery that
the pilot she had been planning to spend a romantic weekend with already had a fiancée tucked
away.

Lola had had her fingers badly burned by the
experience. She would never forget the misery she
had experienced afterwards—because of his callous
deceit more than anything else. And it had managed
to put her off serious involvement, though that had
been easy to avoid—there hadn't been anyone else
she had remotely fancied enough to contemplate
plunging headlong into an affair with them.

Until now.

'You promised me your life-story,' she said hastily, and was slightly nonplussed by his reaction.

His shoulders had tensed as if he was suddenly under stress. 'Did I?' he queried coolly.

Lola sensed his reluctance, and wondered what had caused it. 'You know you did!'

His expression was guarded. 'And what if I told you that I don't particularly care for talking about myself?' he questioned.

'I would say that either you're repressed or you've something to hide!'

'Touché!' he laughed. 'What would you like to know?'

Lola sat back in her seat. 'Oh, I'm sure that an intelligent man like yourself doesn't need any help from *me*,' she told him sweetly.

His grey eyes narrowed suspiciously. 'Are you teasing me again, Lola Hennessy?'

'Why?' she laughed, enjoying herself hugely. 'Can't you take it?'

'Oh, I can take anything you care to throw at me,' he challenged in a sultry murmur. 'Anything at all.'

The atmosphere began to crackle with an eroticism which was almost tangible, and Lola found herself unable to look him in the eye. She began fiddling unnecessarily with the thick linen napkin on her lap, and was indescribably pleased when she decided to let his mocking invitation go unanswered and started to speak.

'I come from Wales,' he told her, and his musical accent deepened as he went on to describe the country of his birth. 'Beautiful West Wales—which is wild and dark and thoroughly magnificent!'

Yes, thought Lola at once. Wild and dark and magnificent—just like you...

He looked at her keenly. 'I'm afraid that it's the classic, corny tale of rags to riches—sure you're ready for it?'

Beneath the flippant tone and the throw-away statement Lola was convinced that she detected a chink in his steely armour and she found herself intrigued by this apparent streak of vulnerability. For surely it added an extra dimension to the man's character, rather than detracting from it?

'Quite ready,' she told him truthfully, and something in her quiet, almost respectful tone made him grow still for a moment.

'My father was a coal-miner,' he began, and his grey eyes darkened with pain. 'But he suffered a lot of ill health when he was still quite young—along with many others, of course.' He ran a hand distractedly through his thick, tar-black hair. 'When I was eight he was finally laid off and given an invalidity pension.' His voice grew harsh. 'But it wasn't enough to feed a family of sparrows—let alone me and Mam and my sister, Catrin.'

He gazed down at the small centrepiece on the table, a glass bowl filled with yellow mimosa, and his features hardened with the memories. 'So my mother went out to work—doing the only things which an early marriage had qualified her for. She cleaned houses, took in sewing—did whatever she could do which fitted in around Catrin and me. Mostly she was what I suppose you'd call a drudge.'

He shot her a bleak, almost defiant look and Lola suddenly caught a glimpse of the boy behind the man. The boy who had longed to protect his mother from hard work and penury, but because of his tender years and inexperience had been unable to do either.

Which must have been a heavy cross for a proud man like Geraint Howell-Williams to carry, Lola recognised instinctively. 'And?' she prompted gently.

'Oh, it wore her down eventually. And him. His pride baulked at having to let a woman support him. The two of them used to go without to give us children fresh, wholesome food, and ultimately they suffered for it. When the flu epidemic swept Wales, they both succumbed to it. I was ten,' he added as an afterthought, as if that fact were somehow unimportant.

Lola was no stranger to childhood pain, and she winced in distress as she tried to imagine his anguish at being left an orphan at such a tender age. 'Oh, Geraint,' she said softly. 'How on earth did you manage?'

She saw the sudden deep lines of pain that scored his face, but they were gone again almost immediately—as though over many years he had schooled his expression so as never to betray them.

'My sister brought me up,' he told her, smiling for the first time, but the smile was laced with something bitter which Lola could not, for the life of her, work out. 'She sacrificed her place at university in order to give me mine, years later—and for that I shall forever be in her debt.' He turned to catch the eye of a waiter, and in profile his proud, craggy features might have been hewn from stone.

But by the time a bottle of mineral water had been placed on the table he seemed to have recovered his usual self-assurance and a frosty light which glittered in the depths of his grey eyes warned Lola that he would not tolerate her sympathy—however well-intentioned.

'So you've heard all my secrets, Lola,' he told her silkily. 'Now I think it's your turn, don't you?'

Lola felt squirmingly uncomfortable at the way he was looking at her. Because it was no longer desire that she read in his grey eyes, nor even a benign interest. Instead, there was an air of detachment about him, a sudden air of almost icy curiosity which made Lola's throat clam up nervously, and it took several mouthfuls of the gin and tonic he had ordered for her before the courage of her convictions returned, and she was able to face him with a resolute air.

'What do you want to hear?' she asked quietly.

'Oh, the usual stuff.'

His voice was so brittle, Lola thought. It was almost as if he had decided that, having confided in her, he now needed to step back, become a cold and untouchable stranger. Was he always so unpredictable? she wondered. 'How jaded you sound!' she told him honestly.

'Do I?'

'But then I suppose you have women pouring their hearts out to you all the time.'

He gave an odd smile. 'I'm not giving any secrets away, sweetheart—if that's what you're getting at.'

Did that mean he was discreet?

Lola wondered sightly hysterically just how many other women *had* paraded their upbringing in front of him like this, on request. Had some of them perhaps embellished their early years, in order to impress him—moulded them to a degree, by means of oversight or exaggeration, so as to measure up to what they thought he wanted of them?

Well, not Lola! Hers had been an unremarkable, isolated and often lonely childhood, but she had always refused to sentimentalise it.

'I spent my early life in a small village called Taverton, in Cornwall,' she told him starkly. 'My mother still lives there.'

'And your father?'

'He died when I was eleven.' Lola took a quick gulp of her drink and then regretted it as the tonic fizzed its way uncomfortably down her throat.

'That's something we have in common, then,' he said quietly. His voice sounded strained—as though the fact was a shock to him, and an unwelcome one at that.

'Yes.' Lola looked up as once again the understanding flowed between them like a warm current, as it had done last night at the tennis club, and she suddenly realised how easy it would be to fall for him. To *really* fall for him.

He narrowed his grey eyes consideringly. 'So you haven't lived at home for—how long?'

'Seven years. I'm twenty-five.' She tried to inject a little enthusiasm into her voice, to act as if this was a gentle getting-to-know-you chat, instead of an interrogation by a master inquisitor—which was how it felt!

He put his glass down on the table and smiled, as if he had resolved to lighten the mood by changing the subject. 'And have you always wanted to fly?' he asked, his eyes never leaving her face.

Lola nodded. Flying had been her whole life, really—and her enthusiasm for it had never waned. 'Always!' she told him. 'I had never even been on an aeroplane before—and yet I knew that I wanted to be an air stewardess right from the word go. I got the job with Atalanta at eighteen, and I've been with them ever since.'

He leaned back in his chair and watched as the waiter placed a plate of tossed green salad in front of her.

'So what is life like,' he asked casually, 'as an air stewardess?'

Lola plunged her fork into a buttery wedge of avocado and scowled. 'You don't *have* to go through the motions of asking me these questions, you know,' she told him defensively. 'I mean, you must have dated stewardesses before—I'd hate to think that I was forcing you to sit through yet another rendition of "what I love about my job"!'

'*Now* who's being the cynic?' he responded coolly. Some indefinable emotion hardened the gorgeous mouth. 'I can assure you, Lola, that I have never been forced to do anything in my life.'

No, she couldn't really imagine anyone having the strength of character to be able to browbeat Geraint Howell-Williams into doing something he didn't want to!

She started on the predictably delicious wine he had ordered for her and allowed herself the luxury of looking directly into the black-fringed, stormy eyes. 'Life as a stewardess is terrific,' she told him. 'I would recommend it to anyone for all the obvious reasons—namely the opportunity to see the world and meet lots of people.'

'And in the long term?'

Lola blinked. 'The long term?'

'Is it a job you can see yourself doing at forty?'

Lola looked at him blankly, trying to imagine herself trundling the drinks trolley up the aisle fifteen years on, and shuddered. 'Well, no. Not really.'

'So what *do* you see yourself doing at forty?'

Lola clammed up. For some reason it would be acutely embarrassing to tell him that at forty she would have hoped to have settled down with some wonderful man she had yet to meet, and be rearing lots of children! 'I—er—haven't given it a lot of thought,' she answered weakly.

He threw her a hard, disbelieving look. 'Really? Not planning to be safely tucked up in the marital bed by then? Don't you want to be married, Lola?'

The fact that he had so accurately echoed her thoughts threw Lola completely. 'Perhaps,' she admitted proudly, refusing to be cowed by his rather patronising attitude. He was managing to make a desire to settle down and get married sound as bizarre as a wish to fly to the moon in a hot-air balloon! 'Why not?'

'Why not indeed?' he responded faintly. 'But so far no one has been able to tempt you away from your single, exciting, globe-trotting life?' he probed.

'No so far, no.'

'But I imagine that there must have been some candidates along the way,' he drawled suggestively.

It was not quite an insult, but it was as near as dammit, and Lola glared at him, her narrowed eyes sparking hot blue fire as she dared him to continue.

'Candidates for what?' she questioned slowly.

'Marriage. Relationships. You must have known a good few men over the years—isn't that one of the perks of the job?'

Lola put her wineglass down with a thud. 'Are you trying to offend me, Geraint?'

'By asking about your men-friends?' He regarded her levelly, the flame from the flickering candle casting fascinating shadows over the chiselled bones of his face. 'Now what could be offensive about that?'

She placed her knife and fork neatly on the plate, much of her salad untasted. 'The implication being that I sleep around?'

He gave her a long, steady look and Lola curled her nails hard into the palms of her hands in a deliberate attempt to distract herself from the power of that gaze.

'Well, that *is* what you were implying, isn't it?' she demanded.

'You're being very defensive,' he murmured, and poured her some mineral water.

'So what if I am?' she retorted, drinking some of the water thirstily. And who *wouldn't* be defensive, she thought wryly, when they'd had to cope with as many snide innuendos as she had that evening? 'Anyway, I've talked far too much. Tell me some more about you.'

'What else could you possibly want to know?' he drawled.

'You haven't even told me what you do for a living!' she realised aloud. '*Or* how you know the mysterious Dominic Dashwood.'

'I deal in money,' he told her curtly, his grey eyes as cold as an arctic sea. 'Dominic I met during my time at Oxford.'

She remembered the small but significant pause after he had introduced himself at the tennis club. 'And should I have heard of you?'

'Not necessarily.' He shrugged. 'Only if you happen to read the financial pages—and then I've been in New York for the past ten years so it's unlikely you'd have heard of me anyway. I've only just come back.'

'And what brought you back?'

Another pause. 'Family business,' he said finally, his face hardening forbiddingly.

Lola took no notice. 'So what does someone who deals in money actually *do*?' she persisted.

His face grew even colder. 'I buy and sell,' he told her tersely. 'That's all.'

Lola registered the superb quality of the suit he wore. Clearly buying and selling, as he put it, was very lucrative indeed! 'You make it sound so simple,' she said slowly.

There wasn't a flicker of emotion on his face as he watched her unconscious assessment of him. 'I prefer not to make it sound anything at all,' he told her flatly. 'But you asked the question, as women inevitably do—'

'Oh, for goodness' sake!' Lola glared at him. 'You asked *me* exactly what you wanted; what did I do that was so different?'

'You homed straight in on the money side of it, didn't you, sweetheart? Sometimes I really think it would save time if I produced a bank statement for women to peruse at their leisure!'

'Oh, *sor-ry*!' said Lola furiously. 'I didn't realise you were so touchy about money!'

'When you've met as many women with dollar signs flashing in their eyes as I have,' he mused with distaste, 'then being touchy about it is inevitable.' He gave a self-deprecating shrug of his shoulders, before he said, 'Were your parents very rich, Lola?'

The deep, velvet undertone of his voice sent new shivers skating down Lola's spine, but she could not quite decide whether it was excitement or fear which had caused them. 'Why do you ask that?' she queried.

His eyes glittered. 'Isn't it rather obvious? Your house on St Fiacre's for one thing. How did you happen to come by a house like that on your salary?'

'How do you *think* I came by it?' she retaliated as she encountered the oh, so familiar judgemental expression on his face.

'A man, I suppose?'

Lola met his gaze and read the condemnation there and didn't care. How *dared* he judge her without even knowing her? 'That's right,' she said steadily.

'A rich man?'

She saw the censorious look which soured his expression and decided that she would like to sour it even more! 'You've got it in one!' She smiled and noticed his knuckles whiten as the bread stick he had picked up was reduced to dust by the inadvertent clenching of that strong fist.

'A *ve-ry* rich man,' she purred deliberately, and saw a muscle begin to work violently in his cheek.

'Much richer than you, probably. Why, I expect he could buy you out a hundred times over, Geraint!'

He let the bread dust trickle out of his hand into the large, cut-glass ashtray, so that it looked like sand running through an egg-timer. His eyes were full of mocking amusement as they caught her in their cool gaze. 'I doubt it,' he contradicted her with soft confidence.

And Lola doubted it too; that was the trouble. She found herself wondering why she hadn't stormed out of the restaurant, but one look at the lean, autocratic face in front of her reminded her that it was not easy to walk out on someone *this* gorgeous. She drank more wine in an effort to calm herself.

'So what was it between you and your generous benefactor?' he asked eventually. 'The love-affair to rival all love-affairs?'

'No, it wasn't,' she answered flatly, then sighed, wondering just how much to tell him. The trouble was that there was nothing much to tell—but nobody ever believed her! Lola had grown used to people who didn't really know her drawing their own tacky conclusions! But for some reason that cold look of disapproval on the face of Geraint Howell-Williams was more than she could bear.

She leaned her elbows on the table and rested her chin in her hands to look at him earnestly. 'I don't really like talking about it,' she admitted.

'Oh?'

Lola glared at him. 'Because nobody believes me, and because people tend to pre-judge me—they all seem to think that I'm some kind of amateur hooker who played for very high stakes—and won! A horrible, critical look comes over their faces—a bit like the expression you're wearing now!'

'Am I? Sorry.' He lifted his shoulders in a gesture of appeal which had something of the little boy about it, and it stabbed at Lola's soft heart.

'Of course the other reason I don't talk about it,' she explained, her blue eyes glinting with mischief, 'is because now that I own a prime piece of real estate I'm very wary of would-be fortune hunters.'

'And do you put *me* in that category?' he asked her softly.

She looked at him with a wry expression. 'Don't be ridiculous!' she snorted. 'Fortune hunters don't usually come kitted out in handmade Italian suits!'

'Thank you,' he said gravely, though Lola thought she detected a reciprocal glitter of humour lurking in the depths of his stormy eyes. 'I'll take that as a compliment, shall I?'

Lola went pink. 'If you want.'

'So why don't you tell *me* all about the house?' he suggested. 'And let me judge for myself.'

What harm would the truth bring? Lola thought. Anything would be better than him believing that she had been Peter Featherstone's lover. She began to pleat her napkin with fidgety fingers. 'About three years ago, I first met Peter Featherstone on a flight to Brussels—'

'Did he have a woman with him?' he demanded quickly.

Lola frowned at the interruption. 'No.'

He nodded. 'And so you got chatting—naturally?'

Lola gave him a long-suffering look. '*Yes,*' she agreed, with sardonic emphasis. 'We aren't discouraged from chatting to passengers, you know. Do you have a problem with that, Geraint?'

His face was expressionless. 'I guess not.'

'Peter used to travel all over Europe quite regularly, and often I was among the cabin crew. And then one day, while we were chatting, quite by coincidence I discovered that he was on the board of a charity I'm involved with—'

'Charity?' he repeated incredulously. 'You're involved with a *charity*?'

'Oh, for goodness' sake!' exploded Lola. 'Now who's talking stereotypes? What's the matter, Geraint—don't I fit into your idea of the kind of person who does things for charity?' She looked at him, and her mouth twitched. 'No, on second thoughts don't answer that!'

'Which charity?' He frowned.

'Dream-makers,' Lola told him, still gratified by the rather dazed expression which had not left his face since the mention of the word 'charity'! 'It's for very sick children. We find out where they'd most like to go, or who they would most like to meet, and we try and arrange it for them. Peter owned a number of toy shops and factories in the south of England and he was a very generous benefactor.'

'So what happened?' he asked carefully. 'Between you and Peter.'

'Well, nothing—that's the odd thing.'

'No romance?' he barked.

'He was *years* older than me, for heaven's sake! Over sixty—'

'But an attractive man, all the same?'

Lola afforded him an icy look. 'I honestly never thought of him in those terms. I only had dinner with him once or twice, after which for some inexplicable reason, he must have changed his will—leaving me the house. And then he died. Perhaps he knew just how sick he had become. Anyway, he suffered a fatal heart attack about a year ago.'

'That's terrible,' he said automatically.

It was strange, and Lola couldn't quite put her finger on why, but she definitely got the feeling that her first impression of him this evening had been the right one, and that Geraint was only going through the motions of responding to what she was saying. It was as though his answers were conditioned, rather than genuine. Almost as if he was asking questions to which he already knew the answers... But how could he? They had only met for the first time last night.

'Yes, it was terrible,' she agreed slowly, but more out of respect than out of sorrow—she had not known Peter Featherstone either long enough or well enough to feel any deep grief at his passing.

There was silence for a moment while he studied her face. 'I'm sorry,' he said eventually, but there was a strained, indefinable note to his voice. 'That he died, I mean.'

'You don't sound particularly sorry.'

'Don't I? Maybe that's because I'm jealous.'

Jealous?

Lola despised herself for the longing that his flippant little remark produced. Even after all the nasty slurs he had directed at her, too! Would nothing keep her from coming back for more? She put on her most bemused voice. 'But you barely know me, Geraint. So why on earth would you be jealous?'

He lowered his voice to a sultry whisper. 'Because I'd like to know what spells you could possibly weave and cast on a sixty-year-old man to make him leave you a house worth a million pounds. You must be pure dynamite in bed, Lola.'

For a moment, she thought that she had not heard him correctly, and then the full horror of his words hit her like a kick in the teeth. Lola slammed her glass down on the table and stared at him.

'What right,' she whispered incredulously, 'what *right* do you think you have to say a thing like *that* to me? *And* after all I've said! *And* after convincing myself that you were the kind of person who could be trusted to hear the whole story! Well, more fool me!' She leaned across the table, and her eyes spat sapphire fire at him. 'Do you think that buying a woman dinner gives you carte blanche to make boorish remarks?' She pushed her chair back and got to her feet. 'Well? Do you?' she repeated shrilly.

'Where do you think you're going?' he asked her calmly.

Lola nearly exploded with rage. 'I don't *think* I'm going anywhere! I *am* going! Back to my hotel! Where else? Because if you imagine that I would spend another minute in *your* company after what you've just said to me, then you haven't an ounce of perception in your body!'

'And if I happen to apologise for my boorish remarks—as you so sweetly put it?'

'Oh!' Lola exclaimed exasperatedly, not caring that the diners around them were steadily growing silent as they observed a very un-English display of public passion. 'Isn't that *just* like a man?'

'It is?'

'Yes, it damn well *is*! You think you can come out with all kinds of inconsiderate, brutish comments, and then all you need to do is to bat your eyelashes and mumble "I'm sorry" and suddenly that makes everything better! Well, take it from me, Geraint Howell-Williams—it *doesn't*!'

'Obviously not.' He gave her a small, tight smile. 'I can see that I am going to get lots of insight into what motivates male behaviour, if I stick around!'

'*Oh!*'

'And now you have two choices,' he said challengingly, without giving her a chance to say anything else. 'You can either sit down and we can start all over again—especially since I *have* apologised...' He looked up to meet her stony eyes.

'Or?'

'You can make a scene in the middle of the restaurant.' He spoke with the lazy assurance of someone who was certain that, once challenged, Lola would back down.

'And you think I wouldn't?' she queried, hardly noticing the waiter who had removed their salads to deposit two delicious plates of pasta in front of them.

'I think you're far too sensible.'

Lola stared at him as if he were completely mad. She leaned across the table again, her hair spilling in mahogany disarray over her pale, silk-covered shoulders. 'There's no need to make it sound as if this whole disastrous evening is *my* fault!' she declared hotly. '*You* were the one who interrogated and then insulted me and *you* are the one who is going to have to learn a lesson, Mr Howell-Williams!'

'From whom?'

'You're looking at her!'

'Oh, really?'

'Yes, *really*!'

He looked amused. 'And what might that lesson be?'

It was the final straw for Lola. Oh, not the mocking tone of his question nor even the teasing smile which curved the corners of that delectably sensual mouth. It was *her* response to him that did it. He had been just about as rude as any man could be, and yet *still* she wanted him to kiss her!

'It's a lesson in taking responsibility for your actions,' Lola told him coolly, and tipped her glass of mineral water into his lap.

He recoiled only momentarily, his reactions razor-sharp as he picked up *her* thick linen napkin and used it to blot up the liquid.

He gave her a long, thoughtful look as he dabbed at the mark on the unmistakable part of his anatomy and Lola glowered as he said, loudly enough for anyone who happened to speak English to hear, 'I suppose that *you* want to do this for me, don't you, darling? After all, it *is* your weak spot!'

Someone two tables back must have heard and understood because they gave a raucous laugh and a cheer and Lola blushed with embarrassment.

Geraint smiled at her reaction, and gave a gentle shake of his head as he said, 'Darling, please don't

sublimate your sexual desires any longer. I give in.'
And he held his palms up in a gesture of surrender
as he rose to his feet to tower rather intimidatingly
over Lola. 'I'll miss the rest of my dinner and let
you take me home to bed since that's what you so
obviously want.'

Lola's fingers twitched. 'Why, you no-good,
conniving—'

'Oh, dear,' he interrupted with a dramatic sigh,
playing to the crowd like mad. 'You just can't wait,
can you, sweetheart?' And in full view of the restaurant he pulled her unprotestingly into his arms.

The crowd went wild as Geraint began to kiss
her, but Lola was deaf to the sounds of clapping
and cheering and blind to the sight of diners peering
unashamedly over at them, their forgotten meals
growing cold.

And what had started out, presumably, as
Geraint's attempt to silence her and subdue her and
to re-assert his mastery after having the contents of
her glass tipped into his lap turned into something
quite different.

She tried to hold back at first, keeping her lips
pressed tightly together, but just the warmth of his
breath was enough to coax them apart. He slowly
let his tongue curl into the warm, moist cavern of
her mouth and the intimacy of this small gesture
made her grow positively weak with need.

She gave a tiny moan of submission, her hands
winding themselves luxuriously around his neck as
she allowed him to press her even closer, so that
she could feel the thundering of his heart against
the softness of her breasts.

She could feel the tips of her nipples tingling with the need to have him touch them, could feel the honeyed ache begin to tug deep at the heart of her, and she must have moved her hips restlessly against him in some silent, unconscious plea for she felt him stiffen with tension.

'Oh, Lola,' he breathed indistinctly against her mouth. 'I want you. Dear God, how I want you.'

The bald words ripped into the falsely romantic little saga which Lola had been busy constructing for herself, and she forced herself to tear her lips away from his, pulling herself out of his arms and staring at him in accusation.

'And you think that's all it takes?'

He frowned. 'What?'

'You *know* what!'

'I do?'

'Yes, you do! Or rather you *think* you do!' Lola glared at him. 'You want to go to bed with me—but you start leaping on me before we've even eaten our main course or our pudding! Why, of all the *cheap* behaviour!' she stormed, as angry with herself as she was with him. Talk about behaving like a complete walkover!

'I think we should go and find somewhere quieter to discuss this,' he murmured, with a swift sideways glance at the rapt diners who were still watching them. 'Don't you?'

'I'll bet you do! And let me guess where you're about to suggest! Your bedroom? Or mine?'

He gave her a look of outraged mockery. 'Do keep your voice down, Lola—I have my reputation to think of!'

The remark was enough to bring her crashing back to her senses. As if the whole room had suddenly shifted into sharp focus, Lola became aware of the silence in the restaurant, of the knowing smirks as people watched them.

She noted the direction of Geraint's dark gaze as his eyes drifted to then lingered insolently on the swell of her breasts against the thin, butter-coloured silk, and she wondered whether the other diners could see the blatant thrust of her nipples as desire hardened them into painfully sensitive nubs.

She lifted her palms to her flaming cheeks for one agonised and distracted moment, then something of her normal spirit returned and she rounded on him briefly, her eyes spitting angry, cold, sapphire sparks at him.

'Next time you ask a woman out to dinner,' she drawled sarcastically, before lifting her hand to summon the *maître d'*, who had been hovering rather anxiously in the background, but who sprang forward at her command, 'might I suggest that you consult an etiquette book first? I'm afraid that your manners are really *much* too brutish for modern tastes, Geraint!'

He looked mildly amused rather than seriously perturbed. 'You think so?' he queried softly, and the velvet whisper of his voice made Lola start having second thoughts about walking out on him.

She had to get out of here! And fast!

'Please find me a taxi immediately!' she said to the *maître d'* in flawless Italian as she marched with determination towards the door, her chin held high.

'*Sì, signorina,*' breathed the *maître d'*, but it was Geraint's murmured comment behind her which lingered temptingly in her ears.

'You can run all you like, Lola, because we both know it won't make any difference in the end . . .'

Lola didn't answer, just ran out of the restaurant and leapt into the waiting taxi, asking the driver to go quickly to the hotel, which he did as best he could, considering that it was a Saturday evening in one of the busiest cities in the world.

She was still fuming when she reached her room, shaking from all the emotion of rowing with Geraint and then being kissed by him!

And all in public!

Lola groaned as she stripped off her silk suit and carefully hung it up, then cleaned off her make-up and dived into the shower, remembering how she had soaked him. And just *where* she had soaked him! What must he think of her now?

No worse than she thought of herself, quite honestly, she decided. Her body was racked by an unconscious little shudder as she lathered soap over one of her acutely aching breasts and remembered how understanding he had seemed, as though he was really interested in hearing what she had to say.

Well, more fool her! That so-called under-standing had been shallow and superficial—there was only one thing that Geraint was interested in where she was concerned, and she was just going to have to make sure he didn't get it!

But what if he came to find her? What if she let him into her room and he started exercising that irresistible sorcery of his and she ended up falling

into his arms and letting him make love to her—
just as Marnie had predicted earlier?

Lola drew herself up short. Was she really so
weak and pathetic and untrusting of her own actions that she was afraid to risk being alone with
Geraint Howell-Williams in case he kissed all her
doubts away? What was she—a woman or a wimp?

Let him come, she thought with determination
as she boiled the hotel kettle then added water to
an ancient-looking teabag. Let him try his damndest
and beat the door down.

And then let him see how strong she could be!

Feeling much more resolute, Lola felt her appetite return and she hunted around in the mini-
bar. She had done nothing but pick at her green
salad in the restaurant.

But a quick search revealed that Marnie had eaten
just about everything there was to eat and Lola
couldn't face waiting for Room Service to arrive.
So she was forced to go to bed with her stomach
rumbling, having consumed nothing more than a
cup of black tea of uncertain age.

Foolishly, and hating herself for doing it, Lola
lay awake for ages, listening to the sounds of other
hotel guests returning from their evenings out, but
Geraint did not come.

Even when her eyelids began to drift down, she
was aware that her senses remained half-alert to the
possibility of his appearance.

But still he did not come.

Poised on the dreamy edge of sleep, Lola was
immensely irritated to realise that her last waking
thought was to be one of profound disappointment!

CHAPTER FOUR

BY FOUR O'CLOCK the following afternoon, as Lola drove her zippy little yellow car through the impressive navy and golden gates of St Fiacre's, Geraint Howell-Williams had been consigned to his proper place in her memory.

Nowhere!

OK, she wasn't denying that there was definitely some sort of powerful sexual chemistry between the two of them—because only a fool would deny *that*!—but clearly there was no future for them.

They didn't seem to actually *like* one another very much—and just because their bodies went into overdrive whenever they were near each other that certainly was not a secure basis on which to begin a relationship!

The yellow car turned into the driveway of Marchwood House with an exuberant little spray of gravel as Lola put her foot defiantly down on the accelerator. She had been looking forward to these days off and she was not going to let her chance meeting with an insufferable Welshman spoil her hard-earned rest!

As the car stopped Lola experienced the by now familiar little sensation of awe as she stared up at the elegant, three-storeyed white house, with its impressive porticos and the two boxed bay trees which stood on either side of the shiny black front door.

She still couldn't quite believe that she owned this magnificent pile!

After managing to unlock the front door—which was a feat comparable to breaking into Fort Knox—Lola dumped her suitcases in the utility room and went off to see if there was any post, shrugging off her jacket as she went and impatiently unbuttoning her blue uniform shirt.

The house was much too hot, she decided, and turned the thermostat right down. She had been advised to leave the central heating on whenever she was away on a trip, especially in winter when there was a very real risk of the pipes freezing over. And although it was March the weather had been unsettled enough for her to continue doing just that.

However, the atmosphere was sultry enough for the house to be mistaken for a greenhouse at the moment! Lola wiped her damp brow with the back of her hand and bent down to pick up the post.

As well as the usual sundry bills and an invitation to the Dream-makers ball in May there was a letter from her mother, declining Lola's invitation to come and spend Easter at Marchwood and telling her she had decided to spend the holiday weekend quietly on her own.

Lola sighed, disappointed but not surprised. As Marnie had pointed out, her mother's visits had been infrequent enough when she had lived in her scruffy little flat, yet in all the six months that she had been living at Marchwood her mother had not visited once.

When she had first discovered that Peter had left her the house, Lola had worried that June Hennessy might be suspicious of her daughter's relationship with Peter Featherstone. So Lola had told her mother outright that there had been nothing of a sexual nature between her and her benefactor, and Mrs Hennessy had, to her credit, sighed with slightly over-the-top relief and believed her.

So why was her mother still being so cagey about coming here?

Lola sighed.

Unless she was challenged directly, as she had been by Geraint in the restaurant last night, she tried her hardest to play down her inheritance. She disliked being envied and envy was usually the overriding emotion experienced by people when they discovered that she had been bequeathed a million-pound house for basically having a friendly smile and soft heart.

But what those people failed to realise was just how much it cost to actually run a house this size, particularly on an estate with the prestige of St Fiacre's, which had such strict regulations governing the appearance of all its houses and gardens.

Lola did as much gardening as she could, but she *did* work full-time, and just keeping the extensive grounds in order was costing her an absolute fortune in help.

And sooner or later, she recognised as the sharp peal of the front doorbell penetrated her thoughts, she was going to have to think about selling up.

She had completely forgotten to put the safety chain on the door, and her mind was distracted as she absently pulled the door open, to find Geraint standing there, his legs slightly apart and his hands on his hips.

He looked like a cowboy, she thought, with that aggressively masculine stance which immediately made her feel all small and weak and feminine. And smitten.

Which was not the way she wanted to feel at all! She opened her mouth to lambast him, but he beat her to it.

'Are you *completely* mad?' he demanded, without any kind of preamble.

His clipped query took the wind right out of her sails, and Lola just stood there, too flabbergasted to respond—and, if she was perfectly honest, too overwhelmed by the sight of him to have the will to do anything other than gaze at him hungrily.

In daylight he looked even better than he had done in the restaurant last night. He wore a cream-coloured silk sweater which provided the perfect foil for the thick, dark hair which curled so invitingly around the tanned column of his neck, and an old pair of jeans.

Lola had once thought that she could not im-agine him wearing jeans but now she recognised that that might just have been her mind protecting her from the prospect of actually seeing him in close-fitting, faded denim which clung indecently to every contour.

Because the pale blue material emphasised every centimetre of those thighs—and Geraint had the most magnificent thighs imaginable, she thought lustfully. In fact, he had the finest physique Lola had ever seen. Finer than that of the movie star she had spotted jogging around St Fiacre's the other morning. And finer even than that of the international tennis star she had served cocktails to on a flight out of Florence last month.

His grey eyes narrowed. '*Are* you?' he demanded curtly.

Lola blinked, still too shaken by the mesmerizing effect of the stormy grey fire which blazed from his eyes to be able to think straight. 'Am I what?' she queried stupidly.

He gave an impatient little snort. 'Aren't you at all concerned for your own safety?' And then, when he saw her look of bemusement, his face darkened even more as he continued his tirade. 'I could have been anyone!' he declared. '*Anyone!* Imagine living in a place like this and being stupid enough to answer the door without even using the safety catch!'

Lola's heart rate had slowed down enough for her to feel able to speak. 'But it was *you*!' she pointed out. 'Wasn't it?'

'You didn't know it was me!' he shot back immediately. 'You didn't bother using the spyhole, did you?'

Lola raised a belligerent chin. 'So?'

'So I could have hit you over the head by now,' he ground out. 'And while you were lying unconscious I could have been in the process of ransacking your house—'

'But the security at St Fiacre's is reputed to be the best in the country!' she informed him with a triumphant sweetness. 'Besides which I haven't anything of value to steal!'

'You don't think so?' He stepped over the threshold uninvited, his cold grey eyes taking in a large Chinese vase which stood in the corner of the hall, and which Lola had been using to house her small collection of umbrellas.

'That vase on its own would net you a small fortune,' he informed her, with a curt nod in its direction. 'The sketch above the fireplace is an early Waterman and those two candlesticks on the mantelpiece are made of solid silver—late Victorian, and rather rare.'

Lola blinked, far too interested in what he was saying to register the fact that he had entered her home uninvited. And he certainly seemed to know what he was talking about where antiques were concerned—which was more than she did.

Peter had left her the entire contents of the house, in addition to the building itself, but so far she just hadn't got around to having anything valued.

Oh, her solicitor had suggested it, but Lola had automatically shied away from the idea. She had already been overwhelmed by Peter's generosity, and to then arrange to have the house contents assessed . . . well, that had seemed like an almost greedy, grasping thing to do.

'But far worse than theft is what else could befall you, if you continue to be so cavalier about your security arrangements!' Geraint continued relentlessly.

He met her questioning gaze with a bleak, candid look and Lola sucked in a shocked breath as she realised just what he was getting at.

'No!' she breathed.

'Oh, yes!' he contradicted her cruelly. 'Intruders have been known to show no conscience if they are disturbed by a spectacular-looking woman. If someone is stealing from your house, you can bet your life they don't possess much in the way of morals. If I were a burglar, I could be raping you, Lola—right now,' he ground out brutally.

There was a short, shocked silence as Lola absorbed what he had said, and it was a horrified and white face which she eventually turned in Geraint's direction. 'How c-could you?' came her squeaky protest. 'How could you say something so crude—?'

'But couldn't I?' he intoned remorselessly, and the sombre expression in the slate-grey eyes made it impossible for Lola to look away. '*Couldn't* I?'

'Yes,' she whispered.

'Especially if you happened to be in the kind of provocative state of undress you seem to be in at the moment,' he continued, a feral gleam lighting his eyes, and Lola stared at him in genuine confusion.

'In my *uniform*?' she clarified rather shakily. 'Hardly provocative!'

'We've already discussed the indecent length of your skirt,' he retorted, and his mouth hardened. 'And don't you know that a lot of men are turned on by women in uniform?'

Lola wondered briefly if he was among them, but that was something she did not trust herself to ask him. 'I've never seen any statistics to that effect,' she responded drily. 'And I really can't do anything about men's bizarre little fantasies—'

'You think male fantasies are bizarre?' he interrupted harshly.

'Some of them—and particularly the ones about air stewardesses! I find them insulting to women in general!' Lola snapped back. 'Uniforms serve a useful purpose in making everyone look the same—and I fail to see how a blouse and skirt could in any way be described as provocative!'

His eyes began a slow, cool appraisal of what she was wearing. 'You don't think so?' he murmured huskily.

'No, I jolly well don't!' Deciding that she would not be intimidated by such a blatantly sexual look, Lola resisted the urge to pull the skirt down over her bottom.

'Not even when the shirt is undone—only by two buttons, but nonetheless exposing most men's fantasies come to life?'

Her gaze followed the direction of his eyes and she saw, to her horror, exactly what he meant. The two buttons she had released earlier in an effort to counteract the sweltering heat had made her whole blouse seem to gape open, revealing the lush and creamy swell of her cleavage.

Perhaps it was the excessive heat in the house, or just a reaction to being in such close proximity to Geraint, but her breasts seemed to have swollen to twice their normal size and were spilling out over the tiny lace bra which now felt uncomfortably tight.

Colour flooded hotly into Lola's cheeks and she saw the grey glint of devilment in his eyes as he noted the blush.

'See what I mean?' he mocked.

'*Oh!*' she fumed furiously, and did the buttons back up with difficulty over her straining breasts. 'You're *impossible*!'

'Put on weight recently, have you?' he quizzed sardonically.

Lola met his mocking gaze and wondered just why she was being forced into feeling that she had to defend herself. She didn't want him here! He was just too big and too vital and too sexy for his own good!

Logic told her to ask him to leave; curiosity prevented her from doing so. 'Just what are you doing here?' she demanded. 'Come to apologise, have you?'

'For what?'

'For your rudeness in the restaurant last night!' she told him tartly.

'Or for my refreshing honesty? Depends how you look at it, surely? As for why I'm here—well, I wanted to see you, of course, Lola.' His grey eyes glittered. 'To talk to you.'

Lola shook her head. Her hair was still in its 'flying' style, with all the curls scraped back into a constricting bun, but by now most of them were threatening to escape. 'I thought that we had said all there was to say last night!'

Now, *why* had she brought up last night? she asked herself crossly. For she had caused the enigmatic grey eyes to light up with that stormy potency which made her heart thunder...

'Did you? I thought that talking had very little to do with what happened last night,' he murmured.

'As opposed to fighting, you mean?' she retaliated unsteadily.

'I was thinking more of the kiss which followed that fight,' he said with a slow smile which, when combined with the memory of that kiss, had precisely the wrong effect on Lola.

The druggingly sweet, aching awareness of him returned, and with it her brain went to mush. And perhaps he was perceptive enough to realise it, for he moved closer...close enough for Lola to be able to see the faint, dark shadow around his chin which made him look so unashamedly masculine...and she found herself wondering whether or not he had shaved that morning.

'Weren't you?' he prompted softly. 'Remembering that kiss, too?'

'N-no, I wasn't,' she stumbled, furious with herself for feeling so powerless. 'I've been doing my best to forget all about it, if you must know.'

He nodded. 'Me too,' he murmured. 'But that's the trouble with making something forbidden—it makes it so much more exciting, wouldn't you agree, Lola?'

'You mean that there is nothing quite so irresistible as temptation?' she returned.

'Not quite,' he returned, with surprisingly gentle mockery. 'I can think of something far more irresistible! But temptation comes a close second.'

Lola knew that she was in danger, a danger she was at a loss to define—even to herself. She heard herself clearing her throat like a nervous politician. 'Geraint—'

'I like the way you say my name,' he told her softly. 'With that quiet, almost sing-song little Cornish burr—'

'I need to shower,' she cut in rather desperately. 'And to change. And I need to shop.' She hoped that she sounded more authoritative than she felt.

'Of course you do,' he agreed, and Lola was horrified to discover her heart sinking with disappointment at his easy agreement. Did that mean he was going now?

What had she been hoping for? That he would haul her into his arms and tell her that she was perfect as she was and that the shower and the shopping could wait?

'I need to shop too,' he said. 'So we'll go together.'

Lola stared at him. 'Geraint—'

'Lola?'

'I mean, there must be *millions* of girls—'

'In the world?' he queried with a wry smile, deliberately misunderstanding her.

'Who would be falling over themselves to go out with you!' she snapped back at him, and tossed her dark head like an excitable filly.

'Yes,' he answered quietly, and without conceit. 'And?'

'So why me?'

He gave her a cool smile. 'You aren't being very honest with yourself, are you, Lola? You are as fascinated by me as I am by you—and it's no good opening those pretty lips to ask me for an explanation why, because I can't give you one.' He shrugged with an impatient little movement. 'I dislike clichés, but for once, here, their use seems to be appropriate. Something happened when we saw one another across that crowded room, didn't it? Something powerful—'

'Something disturbing,' Lola put in, almost absently giving voice to her confused thoughts.

He stilled, his whole stance suddenly alert and watchful. 'So it disturbs you too, does it? This feeling? He gave a short laugh. 'Because I don't like it very much myself.'

'You d-don't?' she echoed, aware of the heavy weight of disappointment which had settled like a heavy meal in her stomach.

'Of course I don't like it!' he almost snarled. 'Do you think it gave me pleasure to make an exhibition of myself in the centre of a restaurant in which I have dined happily and without incident for over ten years? Do you think I enjoyed kissing you in public like a seventeen-year-old who had just discovered sex for the first time?'

Lola's eyes widened into sapphire saucers. 'Then why don't you just leave well alone?'

His mouth thinned into a self-deprecating line. 'Do you know nothing of human nature?' he demanded.

She gave him a steady look which told him in no uncertain terms that she would not be patronised! 'A little,' she answered wryly. 'Working with the general public day in and day out gives you *some* inkling of what makes people tick!'

'So who buys more champagne?' he queried. 'The passengers in First Class or the passengers in Economy?'

Lola gave him a bemused look. 'The passengers in First Class don't pay for champagne—'

'And yet they don't drink so much of it as you might expect?'

'I guess not.'

'Exactly!' His grey eyes gleamed with a steely fire. 'If something is free it's acceptable—and therefore less exciting. Put something out of bounds by either making it prohibitively expensive or banning it altogether and your appetite for it increases—*that's* human nature!'

Lola hadn't really thought about it in those terms before. 'I don't quite see how champagne consumption on the airline relates to—'

'Us?' he supplied acidly.

Lola clamped her lips tightly shut, worried that he would see the vulnerable tremor which hovered around her mouth and threatened to blow her cover. 'But there *is* no *us*, Geraint,' she told him tartly, because in spite of everything she derived no pleasure from saying it.

'But that's just where you're wrong,' he breathed, his grey eyes narrowing to flinty chips. 'There *is* something between us. You know there is. Have you no sense of adventure in your soul, Lola? Don't you think we ought to explore all the infinite possibilities?'

'No,' Lola answered repressively. 'I don't.'

'But if you make something forbidden, then it becomes an obsession,' he told her. 'Doesn't it?' he persisted, with a wry elevation of one dark eyebrow. 'And obsession is not just hard to live with, it's downright impossible. Instead of concentrating on the day-to-day pattern of life, your thoughts become one-track, so that you can spend hours reflecting on the pleasing curve of a jawline, or how sunlight can turn hair into satin ribbons.'

His gaze ran swiftly over her face before he concluded, 'Obsession makes life take a back seat, and that's no good to anyone.'

Lola surveyed him steadily, unwillingly caught off guard by his frankness, his lack of game-playing. 'You sound as though you have a lot of experience of being obsessed,' she commented in surprise.

'Thankfully not.' He shook his dark head. 'Any knowledge I may have of the subject I have gained through observation, not experience.' He glanced down at the pale gold watch which gleamed on his wrist. 'Now, why don't I wait here while you get changed, and then we'll go shopping together?'

'Shopping *together*?' Lola found herself smiling at his audacity. 'Because I—'

'Because unless you go upstairs and take off that ridiculous uniform,' he interrupted in an urgent, smoky whisper, 'I might just do something as uncharacteristic as I did last night.'

Afterwards she would hate herself for asking the question, but for now she seemed to have no control over the words she heard herself using. 'And what's that?'

Had he imagined her to be coy? He must have done, for a cool, almost calculating look hardened the smoky grey eyes and something approaching regret darkened their pupils to an inky glitter. 'Did I underestimate your honesty, Lola? You want to play games with me now, do you?'

'N-no,' she stumbled. She wanted something, yes, but not games. Something more exciting than games. And what she wanted she was just about to get . . .

He reached out and tilted her chin with his hands, his gaze locking thoughtfully with hers. 'Yes,' he said, as if he was answering a question, and bent his head to kiss her.

Lola tried to hold back the tide of emotion which was threatening to flood her with its sweet, relentless waves, but it was no good. One touch and she was hooked. Out of her mind and out of control—just like that. Unprotesting, she let him take her wordlessly into his embrace.

He cradled her in a manner which hinted at protectiveness and yet at the same time he made no effort whatsoever to disguise the fact that he wanted her very, very much.

Lola shivered when she felt the hardness of his hips as he pressed his body close to hers, and found her fingers stealing up to rub distractedly at the broad bank of his shoulders.

She heard the small laugh he gave—of triumph and desire and delight—and she lifted her face to his, not caring whether it was right or wrong, just eager to have his lips on hers once more. To have him rain sweet, reviving kisses onto her mouth...

There was an unsettling, questioning look in his eyes and then they narrowed with the determined glitter of passion. Their mouths were near enough for Lola to be able to feel the warmth of his quickened breath, when, with all the welcomeness of an early morning alarm call, the doorbell pealed loudly in their ears.

CHAPTER FIVE

IT WAS Lola's house and it was Lola who theoretically found herself in the most compromising position. She should have been *glad* of the clanging intrusion of the doorbell.

And yet it was Lola who uttered an anguished little moan at the interruption. For two pins she would have ignored the insistent ringing and just carried on with what they had been about to do.

Kiss.

But Geraint clearly had other ideas.

With admirable composure he let go of her and gently pushed her in the direction of the door.

'You'd better see who it is,' he instructed, his voice a sultry whisper.

Still dazed by cruel longing and frustration, Lola stared up at him unseeingly.

'Or shall *I* answer it?' he prompted, frowning as he took in her wide-eyed inability to do anything other than gaze at him longingly.

Lola shook her head, feeling the silken corkscrews of her hair tickle the back of her long neck. 'I'll go,' she told him, and even though her eyes were focused now she found that she couldn't, just *couldn't* look at him.

Not yet, anyway.

'After all, it *is* my house,' she emphasised fiercely as she pulled the heavy front door open.

On the doorstep stood a woman, a stranger, and yet Lola had the oddest sensation that she *knew* her. Her forehead creased in a frown as she tried to remember. 'Hello?' she said questioningly.

'Hello,' said the woman in a soft, deep voice, and smiled.

She was tall. Very tall. Close on six feet, Lola guessed, with a scrubbed white face and close-cropped brown hair which had hints of autumnal red in it. But because she was almost painfully thin her height seemed diminished. She looked fragile, almost tiny, and was wearing faded jeans and an old camel-coloured duffle-coat.

There was something compelling about her face. It drew one's attention to it like a magnet, and yet Lola could not for the life of her work out why, because it was not conventionally beautiful. The mouth was too wide, the jaw too square.

But her eyes were remarkable. In her pale, pinched face they shone out and dominated like two giant beacons.

Amazing eyes, thought Lola. Chameleon eyes. Now green. Now gold. Now brown.

The woman was looking at a spot somewhere behind Lola—almost beseechingly, Lola thought—and then a dark voice poured its way into her thoughts like honey, and she realised that for all of thirty seconds she had completely forgotten about Geraint standing behind her.

You see, she told herself firmly. It *can* be done! You *can* forget him!

Geraint stepped forward to stand beside Lola, almost as though he were the host, and Lola found herself wondering what kind of image they presented to an outsider, especially to an outsider with such a nervous, tentative look on her face.

'Hi,' Geraint greeted her, in a far kinder voice than he had ever used with *her*, Lola thought indignantly, and her heart gave a sudden, frightened lurch. 'You're Triss Alexander,' he said slowly, and some distant bell of recognition rang in Lola's mind.

The amazing chameleon eyes softened. The woman looked up at Geraint gratefully. 'Yes, I am,' she admitted.

'The model,' he elaborated.

No wonder she had looked so familiar! Lola stared at the woman in amazement as she realised that *this* was Triss Alexander—who had been way up at the very top with all the other supermodels, and then disappeared out of the public eye completely...

Lola frowned. She looked so different. So... Just what *was* it that made her look so different?

Triss Alexander glanced from Geraint to Lola, taking in her heightened colour and her dishevelled hair. 'I've called at a very inconvenient time, I think,' she said, her white face going faintly pink with embarrassment.

'No!' Geraint shook his head decisively. 'Nothing that can't wait.' He looked at Lola, and his eyes glittered with a silent promise. 'Stay. Do. Have some tea.'

'Yes, stay,' urged Lola, cheered by the unspoken message in Geraint's grey eyes.

'I won't—thanks all the same.' Triss Alexander shook her head and her hand moved up as if to smooth a lock of hair away from her pale, high forehead.

And that was when Lola realised why she had not recognised her. 'You've had all your hair cut off!' she blurted out.

Triss smiled serenely, but Lola could detect the sadness behind the smile, and wondered what had put it there.

'Yes, it's all been chopped off,' she affirmed briskly, but she winced a little as she said it.

Lola bit her bottom lip. 'I'm sorry,' she said. 'I didn't mean to come out with it like that. It's just that you look so different.'

'That was the whole point of getting it cut,' said Triss in a new and oddly hard kind of voice. 'Out with the old and in with the new—'

'Are you sure you won't stay and have some tea?' Geraint broke in with a steady smile, and Lola observed Triss weakening very slightly.

But then she seemed to pull herself up short and shook her head again. 'No. I won't. I'll take a rain check. But thanks—maybe some other time. No, I . . .' She drew in a deep, determined breath, like a runner sucking in air after a hard-won race. 'I came to introduce myself, really. I've just moved in next door—'

'Snap!' laughed Geraint, and Lola found herself observing the way his grey eyes creased up at the corners. 'So have I!'

Blast him! Lola thought furiously. He never smiles in that crinkly-eyed way at *me*!

'Geraint Howell-Williams,' he said, holding his hand out. 'And this is Lola Hennessy—whose house this is.'

Triss shook both their hands then looked from one to the other. 'You mean you don't live here?' she queried. 'Together?'

Lola found herself pathetically wanting him to say something territorial like 'No, but I'm working on it!'—but of course he didn't. He merely shook his dark, tangled head and explained, 'No. I live on the other side.'

'Not in Dominic Dashwood's house?' queried Triss, with a look of surprise. 'Has he sold up?'

Geraint shook his head again. 'No. He's still abroad. He asked me to keep an eye on it until he gets back.'

'Why?' asked Triss, with a nervous start. 'Is security poor? I hope not—I only moved in here because I was told that I couldn't be better protected if I lived in a nunnery!'

Her innocent remark caused Lola to go extremely pink around the ears and to stare fixedly down at her shoes as she tried not to imagine what she and Geraint might now have been doing if it had not been for the fortuitous—yes, *fortuitous* she told herself firmly—knock on the door.

'Security on the estate is fine,' said Geraint soothingly. 'Or so Lola was just telling me. Weren't you, sweetheart?'

Lola looked up and met his mocking glance with embarrassed eyes.

'That's right,' she answered stiffly, wishing that he would not tease her like that in front of Triss—she was already feeling dumpy and inferior next to the statuesque redhead!

'No, I'm looking to buy somewhere in England for myself,' he explained as Triss stared up at him with her huge, amazing eyes. 'My staying here is doing both me and Dominic a favour, really. He's due back in a couple of months, and that news usually brings his legion of admirers out of the woodwork! I think he's a little fed up with arriving home to find eager women laying siege to him!'

Triss Alexander clasped her pale hands together, for all the world as if she was about to utter a fervent prayer, and then turned her beautiful eyes on Lola and said the most extraordinary thing.

'By the way, I want you to know that I have a—baby,' she stumbled over the words, her whole face lighting up with a fierce kind of pride, and for the first time Lola could see why so many men considered her exquisitely beautiful.

'But that's wonderful,' said Lola. It was instinct more than curiosity which made her gaze flick to Triss's left hand, to see that her wedding-ring finger was quite bare.

'When you're reasonably well known—or have been—well, people think they have a kind of right to you, and I'm very nervous for his safety,' Triss told them, her expression almost hypnotic as she looked at first Lola and then Geraint, as if committing their faces to memory. 'That's the main reason I moved to St Fiacre's—because security is so tight.

'No one really knows about him—the Press *certainly* don't know! My sister-in-law delivered him—she's a doctor. He's my secret,' she said, and hugged her arms tightly against her chest, as if her baby were there in her arms.

'I'm telling you all this because you're my immediate neighbours, and my mother once told me that if you placed your trust in neighbours then they would never let you down. Is that very naïve of me, do you think, Geraint?' She turned her extraordinary blazing eyes towards him, her generous mouth softening as she said his name in a way that made Lola's chest inexplicably clench with fear.

'I think it's very clever of you,' he answered drily. 'And your mother. No trust so charmingly placed could ever be abused. Your secret is quite safe with me.'

'He'll be well protected on St Fiacre's,' said Lola encouragingly. 'There are quite a few babies and toddlers living on the estate; you should be able to get to know some of them—'

'No!' Triss shook her shorn head with sudden emphasis. 'I don't want to! Not yet, anyway. The thing is...' She chewed on her lip like a nervous exam candidate. 'If anyone should come looking, or asking, for me—or for—Simon...'

'We know nothing,' said Lola comfortingly, and looked up to see the oddest expression on Geraint's face—a mixture of anger and defiance that she could not for the life of her work out.

'Are you in trouble?' he demanded suddenly.

Triss hesitated, seemed about to speak and then changed her mind. 'No,' she answered firmly. 'I'm not. I'm going to be just fine. And now I must go. I've left Simon in his pram—see.' And her face became animated as she gestured to the drive behind her, to where a huge, old-fashioned coach-built pram stood parked on the gravel.

Lola's eyes brightened. 'Can I have a peep at him?'

'Well...' Triss beamed with maternal pride, Lola's eagerness too infectious to resist. 'He's asleep...'

'Just for a moment!' urged Lola. 'And I promise not to wake him!'

Triss gave a wry, crooked smile. 'Actually, he's so gorgeous I don't really mind if you do!' she confided.

Lola grinned. 'You shouldn't have said that!'

'I know!'

Lola ran out into the crisp, early spring afternoon, slowing down to a stealthy creep as she quietly approached the pram.

Inside, bundled up in a white bonnet and soft, fleecy white shawls to protect him against the sharp March air, lay a baby, fast asleep, his chubby cheeks all rosy, a beatific little smile fixed to his mouth.

Lola stared down at him. People brought babies onto the aircraft every day, but somehow this was different. Seeing a baby fast asleep in the grounds of her own home made her experience a sudden ache, a primitive desire to have her *own* baby to hold in her arms.

It took every bit of will-power she had not to straighten his blanket or adjust his bonnet in the hope that he might wake and she would be able to pick him up!

Lola heard footsteps behind her, but didn't bother turning round. 'Oh, he's gorgeous, Triss!' she sighed blissfully. 'Absolutely gorgeous! I could eat him up for breakfast! You lucky thing!'

'It isn't Triss,' came an oddly strained voice, and Lola turned round to find that it was Geraint who had come up behind her, while Triss remained on the doorstep, bending down to retrieve one of Simon's bootees, which had obviously fallen from her duffle-coat pocket.

Geraint's eyes were unreadable. 'I'm beginning to see what it is about you that made a wily businessman like Peter Featherstone leave you this house,' he said unwillingly, in a voice which was almost bleak and held some indefinable note of tension. 'There is something really rather irresistible about a woman who loves children so much.'

Their eyes met, and Lola felt as though she could lose herself for ever in that grey gaze. Her heart beat faster as she recognised that he had paid her the greatest compliment of her life. It would be so easy, she thought, much *much* too easy to love Geraint.

'Here comes Triss,' said Geraint suddenly, his voice breaking into the tense silence like a brick dropped on ice.

Triss moved towards them with a catwalk model's natural grace. The March sun was pale and golden and it brought out the tawny highlights of her shorn hair as if an artist had carefully painted them in by brush. With her big eyes and rangy limbs, she looked like some exotic jungle animal that had wandered into a suburban garden by mistake.

Triss's pale face was animated as she peered into the pram. 'He's wonderful, isn't he?' she cooed, her question directed more at Geraint than at Lola. 'Though I know I'm slightly biased, of course!'

Geraint smiled back at her and glanced down into the pram indulgently. 'That's understandable. I think I would be too!'

Lola experienced the sour and bitter taste of jealousy as she watched them beaming into each other's eyes as if the rest of the world did not exist. And at that moment she could have cheerfully wished Triss Alexander a million miles away.

She gave the other woman a level stare. 'Your husband must be as delighted as you are,' she observed neutrally, and then felt stricken with guilt, for the smile died like a withered leaf on Triss's face.

'I have no husband,' she answered woodenly. 'And no partner, either!' she added, with a spirited touch of defiance. 'I'm completely on my own.'

Lola was aware of the furious look which Geraint was directing at her, but even that could not possibly make her feel worse than she already did. Imagine making a mean comment like that to a mother on her own—even if she *was* a beautiful ex-model!

Geraint shot Lola one final glare before turning to Triss and saying soothingly, 'Please don't feel you have to explain your private life—certainly not to us. You don't have a monopoly on convoluted relationships, *that's* for sure!' He absent-mindedly tucked in a stray corner of Simon's blanket. 'But any time you feel the need to call on a man—if your lights fuse—'

'I can just about manage to mend a fuse, thank you, Geraint!' retorted Triss crisply.

He smiled. 'I'm sure you can. But if you're worried about anything—*anything at all*—then call me. Please. Here's my card.' From the back pocket of his jeans he extracted a small cream-coloured card and, to Lola's surprise, handed it first to her.

'You write your number on it too, Lola,' he suggested. 'Then Triss knows she has allies on both sides of the fence.'

Lola nodded, feeling oddly deflated as she scribbled down her number with the slim gold pen Geraint gave her. If Triss Alexander had no husband, and no partner, then what hope did that give *her* with Geraint?

For it appeared that *he* had no partner either, and when the chips were down wouldn't he prefer to spend time chatting up a stunning ex-model as opposed to a rather buxom air hostess he could scarcely be civil to for more than a minute at a time?

Triss's mouth widened into the enormous, crooked grin which had graced magazine covers the world over. 'Oh, thanks!' she said. *'Thanks!* To *both* of you! And now I'd better get going. Simon will be waking up for his feed soon—and, believe me, I can cope with a tantrum-throwing art director far more easily than I can a small, hungry baby who seems to have me twisted around his little finger!' She gave a happy shrug of contentment, and began to push the pram away. 'Bye!'

'Bye!' called Lola, thinking that she would call on Triss tomorrow and offer to babysit. At least that might make amends for her nasty little remark about husbands.

Triss had gone only a few yards down the drive when she turned to look over her shoulder and said, rather absently, 'You must come over some time—for a drink, or something. Both of you, I mean.'

'Sure! We'd love to,' Geraint replied easily, and Lola was still too stricken with guilt to remind him that she had a mouth of her own and she didn't need him to answer for her!

They stood side by side, watching Triss push the pram over the resisting gravel until she was out of sight.

'I shouldn't have asked about her husband,' said Lola miserably.

'No, you shouldn't,' he agreed evenly. 'So why did you?'

'Can't you guess?'

'Perhaps—but I'd prefer you to tell me.'

She stared at a purple-blue clump of grape hyacinth, nestling beneath the budding branches of the cherry tree. 'I guess I was being territorial,' she admitted reluctantly, wondering if he would turn on his heel and run. 'I had no right to be.'

'You had no *need* to be,' he corrected her quietly. 'I've never juggled women in my life and I certainly don't intend to start now! Anyway, Triss wasn't interested in me,' he concluded with a shrug.

'*Seriously?*'

'Uh-huh!' He looked down and smiled into her eyes. 'Seriously.'

She found that she loved the proprietorial way he spoke and she tried not to read too much into it, but it wasn't easy. She let her eyelids fall, to conceal herself from that searching gaze. 'Geraint...' she began, when he put the palm of his hand beneath her elbow so that she was forced to look up at him, to lose herself in the stormy depths of his eyes.

'You're having dinner with me tonight!' he declared roughly. 'I don't care whether it's at your place or mine, or who cooks it. I don't mind whether we go and shop now for ingredients, or whether we decide to explore the local restaurants later. I don't even care if we go and eat an overpriced bar snack in the tennis club here on the estate—none of that matters.'

'Why?' she whispered, fascinated. 'What *does* matter?'

His eyes gleamed. 'Only that by the end of the evening it will be just you and me. Alone. I want to kiss you again, Lola. But properly this time. Without stopping. In private. Knowing that no one will disturb us.'

Lola gave a distressed laugh while her heart beat in a distracted rhythm. 'You can't seriously expect me to agree to have dinner with you tonight when you have virtually declared your intention to try to make love to me afterwards?'

'Surely I can't be the first man in your life to have been honest and up front about his desires?' he challenged mockingly.

He was the first man whom she had found attractive enough to fear the challenge, but she wasn't going to tell him *that*! And if she blurted out the truth—that she had never made love to a man, nor come even close to it—he would never believe her.

Because men had preconceived ideas about virgins. About how they looked and how they behaved. You could be a virgin if you wore no make-up and worked in a library. You could *not* be a virgin if you flew around the world, had more curves than you cared for and a ready smile which sometimes got you into trouble!

'I could try saying no,' she told him with a quiet dignity.

She saw him tense, saw a muscle begin to work quickly in his cheek. 'You could *try*,' he agreed softly.

'But you're so certain that you'd get rid of any opposition I might put up?'

'Maybe,' he admitted.

'Because you're the world's most irresistible lover, I suppose?'

This clearly amused him. He raised his dark, beautifully shaped eyebrows. 'What's the matter, Lola?' he teased softly. 'Don't you like having your objections kissed away?'

Lola swallowed down the acrid taste in her mouth.

It hurt, that was all; the realisation that he was playing with her hurt like hell. Because these teasing words were all part of the big mating game he doubtless played with lots and lots of different women.

Lola felt as though Geraint was the consummate fisherman, while she was like a big but unworldly fish who was being skilfully outmanoeuvred by him and was in grave danger of plopping plumply into his net!

'Why?' she retorted. 'Do your women usually enjoy having their objections kissed away? If someone objects, then that implies they are *resisting* you. If you then change their mind—however enjoyable the methods you might use at the time to make them do so—then surely that also implies a certain degree of *force*, Geraint.'

He had gone very still, as still as the marble statue of Venus which Peter Featherstone had installed at the bottom of the garden, beside a tinkling fountain surrounded by irises which were the deepest, darkest blue whenever they flowered.

'Never force,' he disagreed softly. '*Ever*. But some women like to offer a token objection, a show of reluctance, if you like, rather than resistance. It eases their conscience. If, for example, they have been brought up to think that sex is wrong, or dirty, or in some way shameful—'

Lola's breath caught painfully in her throat. Had he *guessed*, for heaven's sake? She stole a glance at him but, to her relief, he did not appear to have noticed her reaction, he was so caught up in the fervour of what he was saying.

'And that's the very worst kind of rationale put around by men!' Lola blazed, in a storm of temper. 'Isn't it still used as a pathetic kind of defence against rape?'

Geraint's mouth thinned into a forbidding line, and a glimpse of hostile steel gleamed coldly in his eyes. 'There is a distinct difference between a semi-reluctant kiss which may or may not develop into something more,' he ground out, 'and the kind of brutal assault you seem to have lumped it together with.'

'Is there?' she queried coolly.

'Well, why waste time discussing it? Why not judge for yourself?' he retorted silkily, his eyes darkening, signalling his desire to kiss her.

Lola waited, determined this time not to turn her mouth so eagerly towards him. Maybe if she looked at those delectable lips in a detached way for long enough she might have the strength to withstand him.

He was a master of control, she would say that for him. And she supposed he needed to be, in view of what he had just said. Because if he now demonstrated a tempestuous display of passion towards her then it could not possibly be categorised as fair play, not in the circumstances.

Which was why, Lola guessed, it seemed to take an eternity before his lips were within brushing distance of hers. Plenty of time for her to halt him in his tracks.

But she did not halt him; she did not move at all.

His eyes were narrowed, glittering with the bright, intense light of desire, and yet there was no conquering smile playing at the corners of his mouth. Instead, his gaze swept over every centimetre of her face, thoughtfully, almost ruefully, Lola thought.

He put his hands possessively on her shoulders and bent his face very close, and then she *could* sense the tension in him. 'I generally find,' he sighed, in an erotic whisper, 'the anticipation of making love unbearably exciting, but tonight it seems almost unendurable.'

She knew she should be discouraging him from speaking to her in this rather shockingly frank way, and yet if she did *that* then he might not kiss her. And she badly needed him to kiss her. 'D-does it?'

'Mmm. Don't you think?'

Lola swallowed nervously, but, thank goodness, he did not seem to be expecting much in the way of an answer.

Instead, he lifted his hand to trace the outline of her lips with one long finger, and when they trembled violently beneath his touch she saw him give a small smile. 'Which does rather make a case for prolonging the wait for as long as possible. Wouldn't you say?'

Lola stared at him hopefully. *That* sounded more like it! He seemed to be implying that he would offer her some traditional and old-fashioned restraint!

'I suppose so,' she said a little breathlessly, thinking that if there was any holding back to be done then she rather hoped that *he* would have the strength of character required to do it. Because right at that moment she wanted nothing more than to be locked intimately in his arms—and the rest of the world could go hang!

'It's just a little unfortunate,' he reflected huskily, 'that my body is steadfastly refusing to listen to what my mind is saying, which leaves me with nothing to do except what I've been wanting to do all afternoon. To kiss you.' He gave her a lazy smile. 'Unless you have any objection to that, Lola?'

She recognised that after everything she had said he was giving her the opportunity to stop him, but she didn't need to utter a word—he must have read the answer in her eyes.

He slowly lowered his head, and his mouth blotted out everything with a heart-stopping kiss, effectively silencing her in the most satisfactory way imaginable.

To Lola it was exactly like being given a draught of sweet, cool water after an impossibly arid spell in the desert and she opened her lips beneath his, as though she was drinking him in.

Maybe she was just too fussy but kisses from other men, in the past, had been best forgotten. Either she had felt as if she had some kind of slimy mollusc clamped to her lips or she'd had an intrusive tongue thrust into her mouth in a way which had made her want to gag.

Apart from her ill-fated liaison with the pilot, of course. *He* had been a good kisser—but with him Lola had felt that much of it was cold-blooded technique—expertly learnt but with little true feeling.

Whereas Geraint...

Geraint kissed solely by instinct—as if her mouth was some new, uncharted territory and he was the laziest and most sensual explorer in the world, his lips caressing and inciting her to wind her arms voluptuously around his neck and to deepen the kiss herself with a new-found skill all of her own.

She felt his body shift in response.

'Lola...' he said indistinctly against her mouth.

Lola barely heard him; she was too caught up in the sensations he was bringing to burgeoning life. The blood in her veins seemed to grow thick and heavy and the urgent prickle at the tips of her breasts became acutely sensitive, so that even the bra and thin work blouse she wore seemed as uncomfortable as sackcloth.

'Lola,' Geraint said again, but more urgently this time, and Lola felt him grow hard against her and the blood rushed hotly to her cheeks as she realised that she had moved fractionally in response, to accommodate his surge of desire.

She registered his harsh entreaty and tore her mouth away from his with an effort, staring into eyes which were almost unrecognisable—very dark, and opaque with passion. 'Wh-what is it?' she asked unsteadily.

He shook his head as if in disbelief and was silent for a moment as he fought to control his breathing, before saying huskily, 'We'd better go inside, sweetheart.'

'Inside?' she repeated stupidly.

Did his eyes soften, or was that just wishful thinking on her part?

'It's a little too... public here,' he said quietly. 'Why don't we find somewhere where we can be more comfortable?'

The simple question brought Lola abruptly to her senses. She blinked as she glanced around her, realisation sinking in like a cake on which the oven door had been opened too soon.

They were standing in the middle of the garden, for heaven's sake!

And today was the gardener's day!

'Oh, no!' she cried, and ran back into the house, and was about to slam shut the front door, but Geraint was too fast for her. He was inside before she knew it and *he* was the one shutting the front door!

'Get out!' she yelled.

'No!'

'Geraint, *please*,' she begged. 'I want—'

'I *know* what you want!' he declared passionately. 'And if you deny it I'll know you're lying because it's there in your eyes, as clear as can be! And it's what I want too, Lola. More than anything else in the world right now. You. *You*. Only you. I've wanted you since the first time I set eyes on you, when nothing else in that room existed except you. I want you so much I can't think straight.'

It was an admission not of weakness but of vulnerability—at least where Lola was concerned—and it affected her more profoundly than anything else so far.

She could hardly believe that she—*she*—with her too generous curves and her hair which never looked tidy—apparently had the power to inspire the kind of passion in Geraint Howell-Williams which had given his face such a look of such unbearable tension that Lola went positively weak at the knees just looking at it.

Nervously, she wound a strand of glossy hair round and round her finger in a way she hadn't done for years. 'I just don't know what to say,' she told him honestly.

'Don't you?' he queried softly.

'No. I don't seem sure about anything any more.' She stared at him in confusion, thinking, somewhat belatedly, that he could at least have phrased his desire for her more eloquently than that strained, rather clipped 'I want you so much I can't think straight'. 'Geraint,' she demanded suddenly, 'what would normally happen now?'

'*Normally?*' His voice was soft, with an undertone of danger. 'I'm not sure that I understand you.'

'I mean, if it was someone else you had said that to—about wanting them—what would *they* do?' she persisted stubbornly as reaction set in like a cold chill. 'What's the form for this type of occasion?'

'The *form*?' he echoed softly.

'Stop repeating everything I say!' stormed Lola.

'Then why don't you say exactly what you mean?'

'You *know* what I mean! I want to know what your *other* women do! Do they start necking here, in the hall, and allow you to make love to them on the floor? Or do they slip upstairs for their much needed shower, and then you join them, and...and...?' Her voice tailed off miserably.

He had begun to laugh at her use of the word 'necking', but her bleak little voice seemed to sober him right up. 'There are no set rules, Lola,' he told her quietly. 'I don't have a textbook which I consult every time I deal with a woman.

'As for what would happen next—what would you say if I told you that I had no idea? That the situation is quite new to me? That I have never made a habit of the very public displays of desire you and I seem to have been indulging in—or at least not for more years than I care to remember?'

She turned a bewildered face up to him, and surprised a look of something akin to pain in his stormy grey eyes.

'Come here,' he said softly, holding his hand out to her. And when she took it trustingly, like a child, she saw his eyes darken again—not with the passion of earlier, but with that same odd, indescribable type of pain.

Did he want to confide to her the reason that lay behind that haunted look? Some urgent inner prompting caused Lola to whisper his name, but so softly that he did not hear it—or if he did he chose not to answer—and, still holding her hand, he moved towards one of the double doors which led into the sitting room.

It was a vast room, dominated by soft blues and green, filled with light from the mighty bay window and scented with a glass bowl of narcissi which Lola had placed there yesterday, just before she had left for Rome.

Once inside, he sat her gently down on the sofa, and Lola was half expecting him to join her, but to her surprise—and, she was forced to admit, her disappointment—he did no such thing. He went to stand at the window, to watch the yellow patches of daffodils as they swayed with fragile and tattered grace in the March wind.

He stood there in silence for a moment, and when he spoke his voice sounded harsh. 'What do you think you'll do with this house?' he demanded suddenly.

Without stopping to wonder why he had asked, Lola gave voice to the thoughts which had been bubbling away in her head for weeks now. 'I think I'm probably going to sell up,' she said slowly.

He raised his eyebrows in surprise. 'Oh?'

'It's too big for one person, especially one who leads the kind of life that I do.'

'And what will you do? Buy something smaller?'

'Much smaller,' Lola agreed. 'And whatever money is left after I've given some to my mum can go to charity.'

He turned around. 'You're *giving* the money away?' he asked carefully.

'Yes,' Lola nodded. 'To Dream-makers. I think that's what Peter would have liked me to do with it, really.'

He looked at her. 'Are you really this good and this sweet, Lola Hennessy? Or just too good to be true?'

She smiled at the question which had *almost* been a compliment. 'You'll have to judge that for yourself, won't you, Geraint?'

'Yes. I guess I will.' And he turned to stare pensively out of the window once more.

He was so still, Lola thought suddenly, and so silent, too, his stance proud and magnificently arrogant, the set of his shoulders slightly forbidding. She remembered what he had said about forbidden passion, how his eyes had glittered some secret message at her, and how she had shivered in spite of herself.

How little she knew about him, Lola acknowledged. About his past, or even his present—and she certainly had no idea what was going on in his mind right now.

And yet... Lola frowned. Did she really care? She had known the pilot—or thought that she had—and he had turned out to be a two-timing swine. The fundamental question was whether or not she could trust Geraint not to hurt her, and something beyond logic or reason—something buried away deep in her heart—told her that she could.

As she watched, his posture seemed to alter fractionally—she saw his shoulders and the big muscles of his forearms bunch up beneath the thin cream silk of his jumper and she found herself hungrily wondering what it would be like to be contained within those arms. To be *naked* within those *naked* arms...

He turned abruptly and something in her wistful face must have angered him, or infuriated him, or *something*—because his own darkened and his eyes blazed with some strange, pale fire which seemed to drive a shaft of longing right through Lola's heart as she looked at him.

'I'm going now,' he told her harshly, and Lola's mouth flew open in surprise. It was the last thing in the world she'd expected him to say.

'*G-going?*'

'That's right,' he affirmed grimly.

Lola gazed at him in bemusement. 'But *why*?'

'Because...' He shook his head with barely concealed impatience. 'I can't stay. Not now, Lola—not when...'

Lola noted the incredible tension which had etched deep lines of strain on his face and suddenly she thought she understood, or at least partly, though she did not yet know the reason for his astonishing about-face.

She knew that his proposed departure should bring her a degree of comfort, indicating as it did that he must in some small way respect her, and yet just the thought of him going absolutely appalled her.

Clumsily, with limbs which seemed suddenly weighted down with lead, Lola rose to her feet, painfully aware of the lurching disappointment in her chest.

'Of course,' she said stiffly, but she knew, with an unarguable certainty, that if he walked out of her life now, then he would never return.

He stood staring at her for one last, long moment and then he turned away, and the pain was as intense as if someone had punched her.

Lola's hand jerked up automatically, as if it had been twitched by an invisible string, but the silent movement did nothing to halt him as he strode purposefully towards the door.

Could she really let him go?

She suddenly realised how stimulating she found his company—even when he made her so mad she could hit him; she felt so *alive* when she was with him—never more alive, in fact. And she realised how much she admired his strength, and his persistence.

She thought about the unique and powerful effect he had on her. She remembered the exquisite sensations he had inspired in her—what she had felt in Geraint's arms must be the closest thing to heaven on earth—and he had only *kissed* her, for heaven's sake! Imagine what it would be like if he really *did* make love to her! Lola shuddered.

What if she died tomorrow—would she regret having let him walk out of her life?

Damned right she would!

Not that you could live your life solely on the basis that it might not last beyond the day, because hopefully it would—and all actions had their repercussions.

But what of passion, and living life to the full? Was she sentencing herself to a life without either? Hadn't that been one of the reasons why she had left Cornwall in the first place? To escape from the drab, monotonous existence which her mother had embraced if not eagerly, then resignedly?

What if she never fell in love? Never met the man with whom she hoped to settle down in quiet obscurity, to rear children and grow vegetables? Or should that be the other way round? she mused.

In that case she would never experience the joys of love. Lola sighed. And was it so very wrong to want to experience them? Even if it *was* only once? Wasn't sex supposed to be a gift from God?

'Geraint!' she called out, without any conscious intention of doing so. 'Geraint!'

He stopped, but seemed to take for ever to turn round again, and when he did his face was as cool and as expressionless as if it had been sculpted from marble. 'Yes, Lola?' he queried dispassionately. 'What is it?'

Lola lost herself in that sweeping grey stare, knowing suddenly that all her moral agonising had been for nothing. Because she truly believed that sex, when defined by love, was not wrong at all. And she realised that somehow, on a primitive level at once too simple and too sophisticated for her understanding, that crazily, stupidly, ridiculously, she had fallen in love with Geraint Howell-Williams.

'Don't go, Geraint,' she whispered helplessly into the fraught silence. 'I don't want you to go.'

She sensed some inner tussle as his face hardened, and then suddenly he was beside her again, his eyes narrowed and searching as they swept over her, as if he was expecting her to change her mind.

But Lola had no intention of changing her mind, and even if this was the craziest thing she had ever done she seemed powerless to stop herself.

'Lola,' he said quietly, and she shook her head despairingly even as her heart thrilled at the way he said her name.

'And I don't even know anything about you!' she wailed, as if that mattered.

The stormy grey eyes were turned on her in a steady stare and a hint of amusement lit their depths.

'What do you want to know?'

'Everything!' she declared fervently.

'What's everything?' he laughed.

'Oh, *you* know! The things you like to do...' She began to blush at the look on his face.

'Shh,' he instructed gently, lifting his hand to slowly pull out the tortoiseshell clasp which secured her hair, so that it tumbled in glossy profusion around the pale oval of her face.

'I *will* tell you everything—anything,' he stated unevenly. 'Anything at all. But not now. Not when my eyes are dazzled by your beauty... my nostrils filled with your scent... my body aching to hold you in my arms once more, sweet, sweet Lola...'

It was a combination of the things he was saying and the passionate way he was saying them which made Lola want to throw caution to the wind.

She needed him *now*, more than she had ever needed anything in her life before. And explanations and life-stories could wait.

She swayed against him and he caught her instantly, clasping her close to his chest. 'Oh, Geraint,' she sighed brokenly into his neck, neither knowing nor caring whether this was a decision she would regret for the rest of her life. 'Please make love to me!'

CHAPTER SIX

GERAINT tipped Lola's face up and looked deep into her eyes. 'God, yes, Lola!' he groaned. 'Yes and yes and *yes*!' And without warning he scooped her up into his arms.

Lola had never been picked up as an adult before, and while she was absurdly flattered by such a display of masterful dominance she was also slightly worried about giving him a hernia! 'P-put me down, Geraint!' she spluttered.

'Why?' he queried softly. 'Don't you like being carried?'

Lola sighed, tipping her head right back. 'Oh, yes! I love it! It makes me feel just like Scarlett O'Hara!'

'Well, then, just lie back and enjoy it.'

'But I'm *much* too heavy to be carried all the way upstairs!'

'Let me be the judge of that,' he chided. 'And anyway, how do you know I'm going to carry you all the way upstairs?'

Her blue eyes widened into saucers. 'You mean you aren't?'

'I mean that I rather thought you liked the sound of being ravished in the hallway. At least, that's the impression you gave me a little while ago.'

Lola flushed. 'I didn't—I mean...' Her voice tailed off. Making love was an unknown quantity and all she wanted was the relative sanctuary and comfort of a large bed. For surely the kind of sexual gymnastics he was hinting at would be inappropriate for a novice such as herself?

He bent his head to brush his lips lightly against her forehead. 'I was only teasing you, Lola,' he told her mockingly. 'But I quite understand your having reservations about being here. Shall I take you next door to Dominic's? Would you prefer that?'

Lola shuddered. Prefer to be made love to in Dominic Dashwood's house? No, *thank* you! She could just imagine the hordes of perfectly toned lovelies who had passed through *that* particular mansion!

And in fact the longer they went on discussing things so cold-heartedly, the more self-conscious she felt about the whole situation. She buried her head in his soft, fragrant silk sweater and wished herself a million miles away.

And perhaps Geraint could sense the sudden shyness which had paralysed her, for he dipped his head and kissed her again, full on the lips this time, softly and yet passionately and very, very thoroughly. 'Let's go to bed,' he murmured.

His words and his kiss made Lola feel so dizzy with longing that they were halfway up the sweeping staircase before she realised it.

One of her hands daringly crept beneath his silk sweater and she closed her eyes in ecstasy as she felt that first touch of smooth, bare skin. She placed her palm flatly over the thudding strength of his heart, and she felt him draw in a deep, shuddering breath as her fingertips instinctively moved to knead distractedly at one nipple.

'Mmm,' he murmured appreciatively.

She risked a peep at his face, and saw such a mixture of emotions there—pleasure and longing and, most curiously, that fleeting look of regret again—that she hastily shut her eyes, and did not open them again until she felt the soft resistance of a mattress dip against her back, and she found herself in the middle of the large bed in the spare room, with Geraint lying beside her, propped up on one elbow.

Lola looked at her surroundings in confusion, momentarily disorientated by the anonymous, cream-washed walls and the nondescript paintings of a room which she had rarely been in.

'But this isn't *my* bedroom!' she exclaimed in surprise. There were a number of rooms he could have chosen, including her own, which was decorated in soft, pale greens and peaches, and which she had chosen for its cool neutrality—it was feminine without being at all fussy. But at least he had not chosen to bring her to what she had always assumed was Peter's old bedroom, with its deep crimson walls and its sporting prints and old, polished wood.

'No,' agreed Geraint quietly. 'It isn't.' He shifted slightly, positioning himself so that he could stroke all the wayward curls off her face. 'You're beautiful,' he told her.

'No!' She shook her head furiously. 'You don't have to say that just because we're—'

'You're beautiful,' he said again, very deliberately, and this time, largely because of the intense look which accompanied it, Lola actually found herself believing it.

'And you're still wearing your uniform,' he commented, on a delicious note of anticipation.

The anticipation struck an answering chord in Lola, and she found herself stretching indolently, opening her eyes very wide as she replied, 'Mmm, I know!'

He cocked his dark head to one side. 'It must be a little hot and uncomfortable, surely?' he quizzed.

'Well, y-yes. Funny you should say that. It…is…actually,' she managed, through lips which were suddenly parched.

His fingers moved unerringly to the top button of the pale blue shirt which strained across her tender, swollen breasts, and he stared down at her, a question in his stormy grey eyes.

'I think we ought to take it off,' he mused. 'Don't you?'

Even if she had wanted to say no, which she most definitely didn't, Lola still felt that she would have been powerless to, especially when he was looking at her that way—with that smoky look of passion darkening his eyes, that barely contained hunger hardening his lips.

'Oh, yes,' she whispered. 'Yes, please!'

He gave a laugh of delight. 'Oh, sweet Lola,' he sighed as he trailed his fingers provocatively down to the first button. 'I've dreamt of doing this to you since the first moment I saw you. Dreamt of this luscious, sinuous body and imagined it naked and compliant in my arms.'

It was so close to her own fantasy that Lola trembled with excited recognition, wondering how a man with a look of such stark passion on his face could have the control to take so long to remove a shirt.

Oh, yes, she was enjoying the teasingly provocative movements of his fingers as they grazed over the thin cotton—in fact, she was getting more and more turned on by the second—but she wanted him to take the wretched thing *off*. And quickly!

'There.' She could almost hear the smile of satisfaction which deepened his voice as he released a second button. 'How's that?'

Lola gave herself up to the feelings which were building a delicious slow blaze deep inside her. 'Oh, Geraint,' she gasped brokenly. 'It's so...' Words failed her, and he smiled.

'Isn't it?' he whispered, and Lola thought she detected a faint note of surprise in his voice.

She opened her blue eyes very wide, aware of the first faint flush of sexual excitement which tingled along her cheekbones, finding the way that he was watching her almost unbearably intimate.

She shut them again immediately. Quite apart from anything else, if she kept her eyes tightly closed, then her inexperience would be kept secret from him until the last possible moment—and by then it would be too late for him to stop. Lola had read enough books on sexual behaviour to have heard about the 'point of no return'.

Because although she had claimed to know nothing about Geraint Howell-Williams she suspected that beneath his harshly handsome, swashbuckling exterior there lay an honourable man.

And honourable men did not bed virgins! Not unless their intentions were serious. And Lola was not going to fall into the trap of believing *that*.

'*Oh!*' she gasped suddenly as the third button flew open, and then the fourth, and the fifth. She felt the cool air washing over her heated, swollen breasts and longed for him to take her bra off.

'Oh, what?' he husked innocently.

She shook her head.

'Tell me,' he urged.

'I like it,' she told him honestly. 'So much.'

'Do you? And this?' He watched her closely. 'Do you like this, too?' His finger lightly grazed over her bra, where the hardened nubs were now clearly visible through the silken cobweb of lace, and Lola started violently as his touch produced an unbearable ache deep in the most intimate fork in her body.

She felt the sweet, wet release of desire and her throat dried and constricted and she made tiny, mindless moans of pleasure.

'Yes,' he agreed, as calmly as if he were discussing the price of stocks and shares. 'I can see that you *do* like it. I think you're going to like everything I intend to do to you, Lola. Don't you?'

'Mmm,' she agreed, though she had scarcely heard what he had said. She began to move restlessly as he peeled off her airline shirt and dropped it over the side of the bed and then his hand moved down to undo her skirt, sliding the zip down in one fluid movement.

He used his knee to ease it all the way down her legs until it had joined the blouse on the thick, oatmeal-coloured carpet and Lola was left reclining against the antique lace bedspread wearing nothing but that cream bra, her black stockings and suspenders and a pair of navy blue knickers. Oh, *why* hadn't she put on matching underwear that morning? she asked herself despairingly.

He was still for a minute, and silent, too, and Lola lifted her eyelids fractionally, gazing covertly at him from beneath the lush shelter of her eyelashes, and was staggered and thrilled to see the look of rapt absorption on his face as he scrutinised her partially clothed body with all the thoroughness of a policeman searching for vital clues.

Her knees jerked up protectively to shield her belly, and he frowned. 'What's wrong?'

It sounded so stupid to say it. 'My underwear doesn't match,' she whispered.

'I'd noticed.' He smiled. 'And I'm glad.'

'Glad?'

'Mmm. I like the fact it doesn't match. If you were wearing your most expensive scraps of French lingerie, it would seem as though you had planned this. And I don't want you in underwear which another man has bought for you!' he finished harshly.

'Geraint!' she exclaimed in horror. 'No man—'

But he had leaned over and taken her in his arms and now he started kissing her with an unrestrained passion which drove every sensible thought from her head, and suddenly nothing in the world mattered other than Geraint kissing her.

And when he had kissed her mouth so thoroughly that Lola was certain her lips must be bruised he sought out other erotic destinations. He kissed her neck, her cheeks, her eyelids, and the tiny, vulnerable spot behind her ears, which had her trembling with an ecstatic reaction which made him halt and look down at her with a kind of hungry bemusement.

'God, Lola, you're so responsive,' he observed, on a sultry note of pleasure. 'So exquisitely responsive.'

Lola felt as though she had just landed in paradise, and the way he was making her feel right now drove all other considerations clean out of her mind. Like how abandoned she must look, with her black-stockinged legs sprawled across the bed, and wearing nothing but a few items of flimsy, mis-matching lace underwear.

But Lola knew that she could not just take, take, take from Geraint without giving anything back. Lovemaking was supposed to be a two-way thing, and just because she had very little experience in what turned men on that did not mean to say that she was lacking in the imagination department. She had read the books and the magazine articles about sex which seemed to be everywhere these days. She knew what to do to Geraint to make him purr with pleasure.

She allowed her hands to roam unchecked beneath his luxurious silk sweater, her palms circling rhythmically over the tight whorls of hair on his chest. Her fingers crept their way teasingly over his torso, until at last she let her nails curl like a pos-sessive kitten round each flat, hard nipple.

She felt his body jerk with pleasure. 'Do you like that?' she whispered shyly.

He forced his eyes open with an effort, a rueful smile deepening the little corner creases beside his mouth. 'I love it, sweetheart—but quite honestly I'm so turned on by you already that I think if you threw me under a cold shower I would still want to make love to you all night! Which I fully intend to do, by the way.'

'Oh,' said Lola, thrilled and yet ridiculously embarrassed by his erotic statement.

'Lola, you're blushing *again*,' he murmured.

'Yes.' It was just the shock of hearing him talk so openly about his desires and reactions like that. Her mother had brought her up with a tight-lipped repression which had forbade Lola ever to ask questions about sex. Consequently everything she had ever learned about making babies had been gleaned from a book. 'I suppose you hate it?'

'Hate blushing?' he queried incredulously. 'Sweetheart, you must be kidding! Don't you know that it's the greatest compliment you can pay to a man, to blush prettily in his arms? It makes him feel strong and powerful...'

'I'm sure you don't need *me* to help you feel those things, Geraint,' Lola said mock-demurely, her eyes darkening without her realising it, so that he stared at her very intently and then gave a husky sigh of pleasure.

'Don't I?' he murmured. 'Then what do I need you for, Lola? This, perhaps?' And he unhooked her front-fastening bra with an easy familiarity which made Lola wonder slightly nervously just how many similar items of underwear he had removed in his life.

But she wondered for no longer than it took for the frivolous scrap of lace to flutter unnoticed to the carpet, because Geraint gave her a long, smouldering look of sensual intent then dipped his head, his tongue tracing tiny circles over each aching mound.

'It was the hardest thing in the world to watch you on that aircraft, bending down in that short, tight skirt,' he murmured, his breath warm against her nipple. 'I wanted to take it off so much that my hands were shaking.'

His words only served to heighten the sensations which he was producing with his hands, and Lola felt her body arch from the bed, as if she had received a sudden electric shock.

'Oh, Geraint!' she moaned helplessly as his tongue wetly continued its tantalising little journey, moving steadily but inexorably towards each rocky nipple. 'Please, *no*!'

He raised his head to look at her, just as his mouth latched onto one rosy, straining nub, and Lola found the sight of him suckling her unbearably erotic. 'You mean that?' he said indistinctly. 'You want me to stop?'

For answer she reached out and clung onto his dark head, forcing him to stay there and continue with what he was doing. 'You know I don't!' she protested hoarsely, her body beginning to stir with a new and restless kind of energy. 'You know I don't!'

'Good,' he murmured, his tongue tracing impossibly erotic little patterns around each hard nipple while he teased her with slow fingertips to the tops of her thighs, and this double helping of pleasure made Lola fiercely determined to make *his* body rack with sensual response.

Or rather what she really wanted to do was to tell him that she adored him, that she already cared

for him more than she had for any other man, and
that she had no idea *why*; that on an instinctive
level she knew that he was the man for her, that
she was now almost convinced that she was in love
with him, and that she didn't just *want* to give him
her virginity—oh, no—it was much more than that.
The thought of surrendering her innocence to
Geraint Howell-Williams filled her with a fiercely
primitive kind of pride.

But of course she could not tell him any of these
things—if she did, she was convinced that he would
run a mile! And the last thing she wanted Geraint
doing was running anywhere! Especially now!

Instead, she experimented, her fingernails softly
scraping their way round to his back, where she
raked them up and down the smooth, satin skin
there—hard enough for him to feel, but not deep
enough to draw blood. Even though she wanted to
draw blood... to taste its sweet, dark, sticky
saltiness...

'Shall we take something else off now?' he
murmured.

'Y-yes!' Dear Lord, now his hands were resting
provocatively at the tops of her thighs and Lola
was almost weeping with frustrated pleasure
and... and... his fingertips lightly grazed over the
brief pair of navy knickers.

'What about these—they seem fairly superfluous
to requirements, don't they?'

He began to slide the taut silk of her panties over
the high curve of her buttocks, and Lola sucked in
an agonised breath of longing as he deliberately did
not touch her where she had been praying he would.
Teasing swine!

Well, two could play at that game...

She scrabbled at his belt, unhooked it and discarded it as, somewhat awestruck, she felt the power of him straining against the zip of his jeans. She should release him. Touch him. Kiss him. Stroke him.

But she couldn't.

She had never touched a man *there* before.

She closed her eyes. This was crazy! Maybe *she* was crazy. Maybe she should call things to a halt now, before he...before they...

But if she let him go much further, then not only might he be *unable* to stop—but she doubted whether she would have the strength and determination to *tell* him to stop.

'Oh, Geraint...' she began as her heart pounded a senseless rhythm in her ears.

'Do you still like what I'm doing?'

She swallowed. 'You know I do,' she agreed hoarsely, and parted her thighs in an instinct as old as time itself.

She heard him murmur something shockingly explicit beneath his breath as he finally kicked away the moist silk of her panties, but then he cupped her face within the palms of his hands, looking down at her before saying quite sternly, 'Do you want to stop? I mean it, sweetheart.'

Lola stared up into his gorgeous square, chiselled face—such a strong face—hearing the plea for what it was. His voice only sounded as grim as that because he was obviously holding himself in check, she realised. That much was evident from the rigid control which was etched onto every agonised and strained feature.

At a stage where most men might have tried to sweet-talk or kiss her out of any doubts, Geraint was showing a remarkable degree of restraint by offering to stop.

She shook her head wildly. 'Of course I don't want you to stop,' she whispered hectically. 'I want you to do what you said you were going to do.'

'And what was that?'

'To make love to me all night long,' she prompted hungrily.

'Did I say *that*?' he murmured. 'Well, in that case...'

And, with that, he began to remove his sweater and then his jeans. And by the time he was as naked as Lola and she had allowed herself to touch every single centimetre of him hungrily she was so mad with desire for him that she tried, foolishly as it happened, to take the lead.

And Geraint smiled with pleasure and turned her onto her back quite firmly, and entered her with a power and a strength and a brief pain that almost made her faint away. Then he stilled, his face growing dark with some inexplicable kind of horror, as he said, in a strangled kind of voice, 'No! Oh, *no*! Dear God! You're new to all this, aren't you, Lola?'

Mutely, she nodded and lifted her face to meet his gaze with defiance, at the same time pushing her hips forward for the first time experimentally.

She heard his harsh intake of breath, saw the indecision which tortured his features, and so she daringly pushed again, and again, and each time she moved he filled her more completely, until she felt as though he was piercing through to the very heart of her.

She watched his eyes darken helplessly as he began to thrust inside her—so, so slowly at first, until he no longer seemed quite able to exercise such painstaking control. Then his movements became faster, harder, stronger—tinged with a kind of desperation which was so exciting it was almost unendurable. And he took Lola with him, leading her along a deliciously tempestuous path which defied description.

When pleasure came, it racked Lola's body with its bitter-sweet waves, leaving her almost weeping with an overwhelming sensation which quickly became a warm glow of contentment when she heard Geraint give a strange, hollow moan of fulfilment as he shook with passion in her arms.

Someone had covered her up with a duvet—soft and warm and womb-like. Its feather-softness cocooned Lola's deliciously aching body. Mmm!

She was just about to snuggle back down into the pillow when she remembered the circumstances which had led to her lying completely naked in the spare bedroom in the middle of the day.

She stifled a silent groan, and her eyelids fluttered open to reveal Geraint lying on his back beside her. She risked a peek at him. His dark face was closed and guarded, although there was a heated flare running along both of his deliciously high cheekbones and his eyes were bright and alive—and she knew what had caused *that*.

Lola shut her eyes again hastily.

'I'm not just going to go away, Lola,' he told her softly, then paused significantly as he levered himself up on one elbow and turned to face her. 'Especially now.'

Blue eyes peeped out at him from the shelter of sooty lashes. 'There's no need to feel guilty—'

'I am *not* feeling guilty,' he interrupted coolly, although the note of irritation in his voice was unmistakable. 'Although I must admit to feeling just a *little* baffled.'

Not half as baffled as me, thought Lola, yawning hugely and wishing that he would start kissing her again and stop glaring at her as though she had just committed a major crime. 'Baffled?' she ventured innocently.

'Uh-huh.' A pair of interested grey eyes were trained steadily on her face. 'And I hope that you're not going to insult my intelligence—or yours—by feigning ignorance as to why I might be suffering from this state of confusion.'

Lola sighed. She had rather hoped that he might ignore the subject and that then it might just go away. But that was clearly not to be. 'You mean about my—virginity?' she asked, trying to sound more confident than she actually felt. But it wasn't surprising she felt odd—it was not the easiest of words to introduce casually into a conversation!

'The very same,' he agreed.

'Are you very angry?' she tried boldly.

'That I was the first man for you?'

'Yes,' she answered in a small voice, hating the indifferent way he had phrased his question. He made it sound as though he was just going to be the first in a long line of many. And she didn't want him to be!

What she wanted, she realised, was for Geraint Howell-Williams to be her one and only lover. And the chances of that being the case were pretty remote. She looked down and pretended to scratch at her bare shoulder, afraid that he might see the misery clouding her eyes.

'No, I'm not angry,' he told her as he smoothed a lock of damp hair from her forehead. 'What man in his right mind could feel anger at being given something so precious?' He bent his head and kissed the tip of her nose, but Lola sensed the sadness which lay behind the gesture without really knowing what had caused it. 'Although I am slightly exasperated that you didn't choose to tell me until it was too late.' He stared down at her with narrowed eyes, and frowned. 'Why not, Lola? Why did you keep it a secret from me?'

'Perhaps I wanted to prove to you once and for all that I had not been sexually involved with a man almost forty years my senior,' she said.

He raised his dark, elegant brows in disbelief. 'Rather an extreme way of going about it, surely?'

She found that she couldn't look him in the eye. 'I suppose so.'

'And why me?' he persisted quietly.

Should she tell him the plain, unvarnished truth? she wondered. Oh, not that she suspected she had fallen hopelessly in love with him, but something more socially acceptable?

Lola took a deep breath. 'Maybe I was afraid that you would change your mind and stop if you knew that I was a virgin,' she confessed. 'Isn't virtue supposed to be a big responsibility for a man?'

He nodded. 'Yes,' was all he said, but the look he threw her was a thoughtful one.

Lola summoned up the rest of her courage to ask, 'Well? *Would* you have done?'

'Played the honourable man, you mean, and stopped?' He gave a small shrug of his shoulders, causing the duvet to slither down to his waist, revealing that magnificent torso, and Lola found herself gazing at him hungrily again. He saw the expression, gave a low laugh and shook his dark head very slightly. 'Be patient, Lola,' he scolded softly, and pulled her into his arms.

Her heart leaped as he held her tightly, but his words were far too noncommittal for her to read anything into.

'As to whether I would have stopped, I like to think that, yes, I would have done.' He lifted her chin and gave her a steady look. 'But if I'm being perfectly honest I suspect that nothing in the world could have prevented me from carrying on once we had started.'

'I'm pleased to hear it,' she said demurely, and ran a questing finger experimentally down over his chest until eventually it dipped into the indentation of his navel. She heard him suck in a long, shuddering breath, before he removed her hand quite firmly and held it tightly in his.

'Not yet!' he told her sternly, but his smile belied his tone, and that smile melted every last one of Lola's inhibitions.

She sat up in bed, elated to see his eyes darken as the rosy tips of her breasts stiffened on contact with the cooler air.

As if he couldn't help himself, he lifted his hand and cupped one breast possessively, capturing her gaze intently as his finger flicked provocatively over an exquisitely sensitive nipple.

'I'm going to suckle you later, sweet Lola,' he murmured, and snaked his tongue slowly over his lips as if to illustrate the promise.

Lola gasped aloud at the expression in his eyes and the slick, moist look of his mouth and the feel of his hand intimately stroking her breast. Excitement devoured her completely as she felt the hot bubble of desire burst into rampant life. She looked deep into his eyes and commanded softly, 'Why wait? Why not now?'

For a split second he looked as overwhelmed as she felt, and then he dipped his head, taking the nipple into his mouth as sweetly as he had promised, his free hand roaming over her belly and beyond, until he had delved into the silken depths between her parted legs.

Lola gasped again and fell back helplessly against the pillow as he moved to lie above her, and it came as no shock to discover that he was aroused.

So incredibly aroused...

Lola wriggled her hips impatiently, longing for the newly discovered and sweet release of sex, but longing more than anything for Geraint to possess her—because in that most basic communion Lola had felt more complete than she had ever done before.

'Oh, sweetheart,' he whispered into her ear, and entered her with such a bold, hard sweep of passion that Lola's eyes widened with pleasure and thought became impossible, and all that was left in its place was feeling.

CHAPTER SEVEN

WHEN Lola awoke, Geraint had gone, and she looked around the room, feeling abandoned, until she saw that the carpet was still littered with some of his discarded clothes, which meant that he had not gone very far.

She went pink with remembered pleasure as she saw his silk sweater, which he had obviously hurled across the room without thinking. She had rather liked the way that his customary sang-froid seemed to have deserted him when she had lain on the bed silently watching him remove his clothes.

From the wicked glitter in his grey eyes, Lola had suspected that he intended to disrobe as slowly and seductively as possible, but in the end he had torn his clothes off with an impatience which had touched her heart as well as her body.

Lola plumped up several pillows and settled back against them, staring out of the window into the star-studded darkness and wondering whether lovemaking just carried on getting better and better like that.

And if that *was* the case, then how did people *bear* the pleasure? How could they lead normal lives knowing that such amazing rapture was theirs for the asking?

She heard the distant chinking of china, and footsteps approaching, and then Geraint appeared in the doorway carrying a loaded tray, naked save for a pair of faded jeans of which he hadn't even bothered doing up the top button.

Lola gulped. With his tar-dark hair all ruffled from where she had been frantically running her hands through it, and the faint sheen which clung to his bare, lightly tanned skin he looked absolutely gorgeous.

In bed he had been the complete lover—passionate, considerate, imaginative...a little bit wild. Lola trembled. Even funny. She loved him; she knew that—it was impossible *not* to love him. Was there any chance, she wondered, that Geraint could grow to love her too?

'Hello,' he said softly.

'Hello.' She smiled happily. 'You look like a rock star in that get-up!'

'And you look like a naked nymph,' he murmured.

'Do I?' she asked him, her smile widening as he approached.

She had plumped up his pillows too, and now she stared up at him expectantly, her face growing pink with the anticipation of having him naked in her arms again. 'Aren't you coming back to bed?' she asked him, thinking how husky and provocative her voice sounded.

'No. Not just now,' he answered quickly, his body tensing—as though she had said something vaguely obscene.

Lola frowned, feeling puzzled. She saw the faintly guarded expression which had crossed his face and wondered what had caused it. What were the rules for after-bed behaviour between two people who did not, she realised with a slowly sinking heart, even know each other terribly well?

Surely it wasn't too pushy to ask your lover to come back to bed with you? Especially since they had spent the most uninhibited hours of her life together, and he had positively encouraged her to tell him exactly what she wanted him to do to her— even when half the time she hadn't even known herself! So was she now suddenly supposed to start playing it cool?

Lola grimaced. She hated playing games. She suspected that was one of the main reasons why she had dated men so infrequently—because she had a habit of saying what she actually meant. And a lot of men, it seemed, found it difficult to cope with the truth!

She forced herself to look with interest at the contents of the tray he had placed on the window-seat. 'What have you brought?' she asked.

'Tea. Wine. Sandwiches. Cake. And some cold chicken and salad I found in the fridge—take your pick.'

Lola adopted a resolutely cheerful tone. 'And what's that supposed to be? Tea or dinner?'

'Either. We've missed both.'

Lola's eyes widened. 'Good grief! What time is it?'

'Getting on for nine.'

'You mean we've been . . . I mean—'

He cut across her discomfiture with a rueful glance. 'Yes, Lola—we've been in bed for almost four hours. Aren't you hungry?'

She stared at him miserably. 'I might be, if you'd only come back to bed—it's awfully lonely in here.'

He did not answer immediately, but went abruptly over to the window and stood staring out into the empty night, before drawing the heavy velvet drapes and shutting out the starlight. 'Why don't we eat something first?' he suggested.

If he hadn't had such a grim expression ruining a perfectly handsome face, then Lola might have made a joke about the condemned man being given a last meal—because that was exactly what the atmosphere felt like. But she didn't even *dare* joke about it.

She was frightened. Frightened by the cold, distant expression on his face and frightened by the physical distance he was putting between the two of them.

But Lola knew that she had to take it like a woman. If Geraint was now regretting having made love to her, then nothing she could say or do could possibly change his mind.

If he had decided, for whatever reason, that she was not the kind of person he wanted to have a relationship with, then she must just accept that—and gracefully, too. So that whenever he remembered her—*if* he remembered her—he would remember her dignity and calmness and not just the way she had blatantly invited him to make mad, passionate love to her!

She chewed on her bottom lip anxiously and wondered just how she had had the gall to ask him outright like that!

'What would you like?' he asked politely, as if he had just met her for the first time.

Lola bit back the desire to scream, and instead said, very calmly, 'I'll have one of those sandwiches, please.'

'Coming up.' He put the sandwiches on two plates, then handed her one—a beautiful bone-china plate in deep green, overlaid with a delicate lily-of-the-valley design, which Lola had never seen before.

'Where did you find these?' she queried as she took the plate from him. 'Or did you go next door to Dominic's and bring them?' Even to her own ears the question sounded ridiculous.

He seemed to change his mind about his sandwich, and put the plate down quickly, as if it were made of hot metal. 'No, I didn't go next door. The plates were here,' he said slowly. 'In the china cupboard.'

'The china cupboard?' asked Lola, screwing her nose up in bemusement. 'Here?'

He nodded. 'Along the corridor that runs from the cellar—you know? There's a doorway just at the back . . .'

She knew the part of the house to which he was referring—the basement area which looked as though it could be used as the set for a Gothic horror film. She had been in there *once*—very briefly. It was dark and dingy and it gave her the creeps.

'I never use it,' Lola said as she eyed the sandwich without enthusiasm, and then something else occurred to her. 'So how come you know more about my house than I do?' she demanded half-jokingly.

There was a silence, but it was not the tranquil hush born of easy companionship. Instead, it was a tense, uneasy silence, made all the more ominous by the bleak, haunted expression on Geraint's face.

'There's something you're not telling me, isn't there, Geraint?' Lola put the plate down on the beside table with a clatter and looked at him, noticing that her voice was suddenly sounding very unsteady.

There was only a fractional pause this time. 'Yes, there is,' he said grimly. 'And it's about time you heard it.'

The fear which was building a bigger barrier between them second by second made her hold her hands up to him in appeal. 'No, Geraint,' she said flatly. 'Not yet.'

She felt at a disadvantage and she was scared. Scared because she instinctively dreaded that he was about to tell her something which would, by necessity, change the whole nature of their relationship. And disadvantaged because she was about to hear what she suspected would be a kind of true confession and she wasn't even wearing any clothes!

She ran her fingers through the tangled mess of dark curls which fell over her shoulders and, thankfully, a few stray locks fell to conceal her breasts. 'Is this something you could tell me in one sentence, Geraint?'

He gave a weary shake of his head. 'No.'

'Then I need to put some clothes on first.'

'Yes, of course. Here.' He bent to retrieve her stockings and panties and bra, and held them out to her in a crumpled array of different silks and lace, but Lola shook her head hurriedly and it took all her determination not to recoil from them.

She wanted something clean and fresh to wear, something which did not remind her of the four hours she had just spent in bed with Geraint Howell-Williams.

'I meant my jeans,' she said. 'And I ought to shower—'

'*No!*' His response rang out decisively around the room.

'No?' Had he actually said *no*? Lola raised her eyebrows at him coldly. 'I know I've just been to bed with you, but I'm not *quite* your chattel yet, Geraint!'

'Don't be so damned stupid!' he snapped.

'Then don't *you* be so damned cavalier! Telling me I can't shower, indeed—and *in my own house*!' she added, on a puff of derision. 'Wait here, and I'll be back.'

'How long will you be?'

'However long it takes,' she answered coolly, without a backward glance.

She marched straight along the corridor to her bedroom, where the pale, subtle greens and peaches of the walls and drapes for once failed to soothe her.

She did not take long; she could not bear to prolong the agony of waiting any longer than was necessary. Something in his expression had warned her that she was about to face an unpalatable truth.

So she showered quickly and felt a million times better afterwards for having done so, even though she hadn't washed her wild, unruly hair. Then she threw on a pair of black denims and a thick black woollen jumper, brushed her hair quickly and clipped it back from her face on both sides.

She stole a swift glance in the mirror, thinking how pale her face looked against the background of the black clothes she wore. Had she subconsciously dressed in mourning? she wondered wryly.

When she went back into the room, Geraint was standing where she had left him, as if someone had cast a spell and turned him to stone.

She took a deep breath and asked him the question she had been rehearsing over and over in the shower. 'Are you trying to tell me you're married, Geraint?'

'*Married?*' He looked taken aback, and then he laughed—but it was a short, humourless laugh. If it hadn't been a contradictory description, then Lola might have said it was an angry laugh. But there was no such thing, surely?

'No, I'm not married,' he told her tersely, and went over to the table on which he had placed the tray, poured two cups of tea, and handed her one.

Lola shook her head. 'I don't want it.'

'I think you should drink it,' he said.

Lola's eyes glittered. 'I don't want it,' she repeated stubbornly.

He looked into her eyes for a moment, then nodded, took his tea over to the window-seat and sat down, although Lola noticed that his own cup went untouched.

'How do you know all about this house?' she asked him quietly, having remembered other things, too. 'The paintings and the vase and now the china storeroom. Did you know Peter Featherstone?'

'I knew *of* him,' he answered. 'And I had met him on several occasions.'

'So?'

'He was my sister's lover,' he explained starkly.

Confused, Lola searched in her mind for the name he had surely mentioned at the restaurant in Rome. The woman he clearly adored, who had looked after him when their parents had died. Who had sacrificed her place at university in order to support him. 'Catrin?' she ventured hesitantly.

He raised his eyebrows in surprise. 'That's right. Catrin had an affair with Peter Featherstone for almost fifteen years.'

Fifteen *years*? Lola blanched. 'What kind of affair?'

He shrugged. 'Like any other long-term relationship, I guess. She's a successful businesswoman in her own right—she travels extensively, as did Peter. She has a flat in London—which Peter bought for her.'

'But Catrin wanted more, did she?'

His mouth tightened with anger. 'Why *shouldn't* she want more? This house was the major part of his inheritance. They had shared a life together for nearly fifteen years!'

'And why did they never marry?'

'Peter didn't want to. No reason—or at least he gave no reason to Catrin. He said that they were happy as they were, so why change? He used to give her that line— "if something's not broken why mend it?"'

'Did she love him?'

'Very much,' he answered reluctantly.

'And did he love her?'

He froze, his features starkly defined and vaguely threatening, and at that moment Lola thought that he looked like the devil incarnate. 'She *thought* he loved her,' he responded quietly. 'In fact, she was certain of it.'

'Then why leave *me* the house?' she wondered aloud.

His mouth hardened into a grim line. 'Exactly.'

Lola stared at him, at the cold, forbidding expression on his face, and indignation slowly began to blaze away inside her. Who did he think he was—implying that *she* was at fault? 'I think you have some explaining to do, Geraint.'

'Such as?'

She stared at him, at where he sat on the other side of the room, and an air of disquiet seemed to descend on her. He seemed so distant now; almost a stranger. Had they really shared kisses and giggles and intimacies all that time in bed together?

She was afraid to answer his question, afraid to put into words her most basic fears, in case they turned out *not* to be fantasy. But if she did not confront her fears—what then?

'You living next door,' she said slowly. 'That isn't just coincidence, is it?'

He held her gaze steadily. 'No. Dominic is my oldest friend. We meet up as often as our schedules allow.' His eyes glittered. 'He rarely uses this house, and when I explained the situation to him—'

'And just *how* did you explain the *situation* to him?' she cut in brutally.

He did not flinch under her accusing stare. 'I didn't lie, if that's what you're implying. I told him that I was interested in meeting the woman who I felt had done my sister out of something I considered to be rightfully hers.'

'And he agreed, did he, to what *some* men might have considered a rather bizarre request?'

'Not Dominic.' He shrugged dismissively. 'He didn't consider the request bizarre at all—why should he? He understood my concern.'

The first arrow had pierced her heart, and she braced herself to withstand a whole quiverful of them. 'And our meeting—that night we met at the tennis club—was that engineered too?' Say no, she prayed silently. Please say no.

For the first time, he looked uncomfortable, but again he did not attempt to avoid her gaze. 'I went there with the intention of meeting you, yes.'

Lola took her cup and drank some tea, and just that one small activity kept her in check, prevented her from some rash, illogical action against him which she might later regret. 'So all that eyes across a crowded room stuff, which you've waxed lyrical about ever since—that was just so much moonshine, was it? You know, you're really a very good actor, Geraint—'

'No, Lola!' His voice sounded savage now, teetering on the edge of control. 'I went to the clubhouse with the intention of meeting you, yes, but—'

'But what? With what goal in mind?' she demanded acidly. 'Revenge, I presume? A desire to seek some kind of redress for the sister you considered to have been done out of her rightful inheritance? Isn't that it?'

'At first, yes,' he admitted. 'Although I hadn't really thought it through properly. Catrin was upset at Peter's death, and I was angry. It was too easy to put you into the category of being a young and manipulatively beautiful seductress who had persuaded Peter Featherstone to leave his house to you.' His voice deepened. 'And then I met you—'

'Oh, *please*!' Lola turned away from him in disgust and sucked a dry, painful breath into her lungs. 'Spare me the sweeteners, Geraint—I really don't think I'm in the mood to stomach them right now!'

'Lola, please listen to me—'

She whirled round, her face contorted with anger and shame. 'No, I *won't* listen to you! I've listened enough and I'm sick to my stomach! In fact, you can damned well listen to *me*! You can say what you want about not having thought things through, but I don't believe you!

'You walked into the tennis club that night, took one look at me and decided that turning the charm on was a sure-fire way of getting me to fall under your spell! You did that knowing that you are an extremely good-looking man who probably never needs to even lift a finger to get any woman to come running!

'And as for someone like me, someone who isn't used to dealing with men like you, well . . .' she gave him a sad, wistful smile ' . . . I never really stood a chance, did I?'

'Lola, it wasn't *like* that—'

'Yes, it was!' she yelled. 'You know damned well it was! Admit it, Geraint! At least be man enough to admit it to me!'

There was silence, a fraught, angry silence as they eyed each other warily.

Eventually he spoke. 'Revenge may have been at the forefront of my mind at the very beginning. I admit that the idea of me blindly reaching out for some form of primitive retribution was extremely gratifying—but that was nothing more than a temporary form of madness. Very temporary. And I can assure you that once I saw you—'

'Oh, please don't insult me by pretending that you were bowled over by my heart-stopping beauty!' Lola snarled. 'Although I suppose you must have been grateful that I didn't resemble the back end of a bus! I mean, how would you have coped with bedding me if that had been the case, Geraint, huh? What would you have done then? Insisted that the seduction should go ahead as planned? Just closed your eyes and reminded yourself that revenge was sweet?'

'Don't be so disgusting!'

'I'll be anything I damned well like!' she retorted hotly.

'Are you suggesting that revenge was the *only* reason I went to bed with you?' he queried in a slow, dangerous voice.

'What else am I supposed to think? I should imagine that for a man who is as sexually experienced as you obviously are one extra notch on the bedpost would be neither here nor there, would it? And, of course, you were working on the theory that I would fall hopelessly in love with you. That *would*, I suppose,' she added, almost reflectively, 'make giving me the push so pleasurable. Only I expect that in your wildest dreams you did not expect to hit the jackpot, did you, Geraint?'

He had gone very still, a faint but unmistakable line of distaste hardening the sensual curves of his mouth. 'The jackpot?' he queried. 'I'm not sure that I understand what you mean, Lola.'

She suspected that she was going too far, maybe already *had* gone too far, but she was in too deep now to stop, on a roll, the words too steeped in bitterness to be halted. 'Me,' she explained simply. 'The jackpot.' And, seeing his still uncomprehending look, she lanced home her point with the addition of a cruel smile. 'I mean, if you're going to try to hurt someone...if you're going to bed them in order to dump them...then what better subject to choose than a virgin?'

He had gone very white, his grey eyes blazing with contemptuous fire as he looked at her in bitter disbelief. 'As I recall,' he drawled deliberately, 'it was *me* who was just about to leave and *you* who *begged* me to stay.'

How dared he? Lola stared back. How *dared* he stand there looking as if *he* was the one who had been wronged and made a complete and utter fool of? 'Yes, and more fool me!' she stormed. She looked into his eyes and was suddenly flooded with a violent urge to seek her own form of revenge— and, what was more, she knew the perfect way to go about it! 'And what if I'm pregnant?' she asked quietly.

He threw her a ruthless smile. 'But we didn't have unprotected sex, Lola—remember?'

She willed the blush to stay away but it seemed to take great delight in flooding her cheeks with a hot pink colour.

Oh, yes, she could remember all right—how Geraint had reached into the back pocket of his jeans for the kind of small foil packet she had only ever seen on sale in chemist shops and ladies' lavatories. She had shivered slightly as it had brought the reality of what she was about to do crashing home to her, and her feelings at the time had wavered between relief that he was obviously sensible enough to prevent any unwanted pregnancy occurring and disillusionment that he had been so prepared. Did he always carry condoms, she had wondered disappointedly, or had he just been so sure that she would capitulate?

But then his mouth had come down hungrily to seek out all the erotic places of her body, and Lola had given up caring.

Until now.

She glared at him. 'No, we did *not* have unprotected sex,' she agreed cuttingly. 'But the method we used is not guaranteed to be one hundred per cent effective, is it?' she ground out. 'As far as I am aware abstinence is the only technique which can lay claim to *that*!'

If she had thought he was white before, she had been exaggerating, because now his face looked absolutely bloodless. 'What are you saying?' he asked, in a voice which was so tightly controlled that it sounded as though it might snap at any minute.

'I'm saying that I am right in the middle of my cycle!' she lied shamelessly. 'I'm saying that, although it's a very small chance, I *could* be pregnant! And what price your petty revenge then, Geraint?'

There was a pause, and when he spoke again his face had resumed something of its normal colour, though the chilly light which glittered from his eyes made Lola want to slink out of the room in shame.

'We could stand here trading insults all day,' he told her frostily. 'But there seems little point. And there's certainly no point in my staying.'

He pushed his teacup away and stood up, and he looked so formidably tall and strong and powerful that Lola knew an aching and desolate sense of despair, but somehow she managed to keep it from her face.

All Geraint would see would be that proud little look of indifference she had plastered all over her features. 'No,' she agreed. 'No point at all.'

'Perhaps you'd like to inform me if there are any—' his mouth tightened '—*repercussions*.' He must have seen her bewildered expression for he added harshly and angrily, as though the words cost him a huge effort, 'If you *do* happen to be pregnant, I will, of course, stand by you in whatever capacity you might wish—'

But he broke off mid-sentence, as if he was too appalled to continue, and, with a curt yet courteous nod of farewell—like a character from a costume drama—he strode out of the room.

Lola heard him going downstairs, but she did not hear the front door slam nor the gravel crunch beneath his firm step—because her broken-hearted sobs drowned out everything else.

CHAPTER EIGHT

LOLA woke next morning with swollen, gritty eyes and a dull ache where her heart used to be.

Now what? she asked herself as she picked up her wristwatch to discover that it was almost ten o'clock.

She showered and dressed and went downstairs to the kitchen where she made herself some real coffee in a vain attempt to cheer herself up. She poured herself a steaming mugful and sat at the table, gazing out at a forlorn-looking garden, the rain, which was pelting down, plastering daffodils to the sodden grass.

It was at times like this that she wished she had a normal job. With normal hours. So that for eight hours a day at least she could immerse herself in some mind-numbing tasks which might enable her to forget the conniving Geraint Howell-Williams.

But it was a futile hope. She now had six empty days looming ahead of her before she was due to fly again. Six days which stretched before her like a prison sentence. Except that while a prisoner would be dreaming of freedom she was doing her utmost not to dream of Geraint.

Which appalled her.

How could she give a second thought to a man who had so heartlessly seduced her? Who had taken her virginity without a qualm, motivated by an emotion as base as revenge?

He was a man she must now learn to hate, to ruthlessly erase from her heart and her mind—certainly not a man to dream of longingly.

Lola shuddered as she remembered her shock at discovering a tiny bruise on one aching breast in the shower this morning. Had that dark flowering been produced by the sweet way he had suckled her?

What if she really *was* pregnant? It was extremely unlikely, true, but stranger things had happened.

And why didn't the thought of a baby produce stark horror—instead of a kind of wistful yearning?

The sharp ring of the doorbell had Lola pushing her coffee-mug away and then frantically running over to the mirror to check her appearance.

Ghastly!

Her red eyes made her look as though she was about to audition for the leading role in *Dracula* and her usually healthy, glowing skin was as white as paper. Well, that was just too bad! She hoped that Geraint recognised that *he* was the person responsible for making her look like a ghoul—perhaps it might make him feel an uncomfortable pang of guilt!

She pulled the front door open, her belligerent expression dying immediately when she saw that it was not Geraint who stood there but Triss Alexander, and, what was more, that the leggy ex-model was carrying her sleeping baby, cradled tightly against her shoulder.

'Hi,' Triss said tentatively, her enormous eyes sweeping over Lola's pinched expression. 'How are you?'

There was no point in lying when her face must have given her away. 'Awful!' said Lola, then wound a strand of hair around her finger. 'I'm sorry I asked about your partner yesterday,' she said quietly. 'It must have seemed pointed and prying.'

Triss shook her head. 'It doesn't matter—honestly. It's a perfectly natural question to ask—I just happen to be very touchy about the subject, that's all.'

'Would you like some coffee?' asked Lola.

'Oh, I'd love some! But if I'm intruding...' Triss peered questioningly over Lola's shoulders.

'No, you're not intruding. Come in. What shall we do with Simon?'

'How about if we take some cushions into the kitchen?' suggested Triss. 'Then we can make him a makeshift bed up and he won't disturb us while we're drinking our coffee.'

Lola grabbed an armful of cushions from the sitting room and then the three of them trooped into the kitchen, where Triss handed Simon over to Lola while she crouched down to create a little nest for him.

Lola stroked Simon's dark, downy head with a gentle finger and thought of Geraint, and had to will herself not to cry as she handed him back to his mother, who snuggled him down and covered him with a blanket.

'He's so good,' Lola cooed. 'He hasn't stirred once.'

Triss laughed. 'That's because he kept me awake most of the night—he's teething. Believe me, he's not quite the angel he sometimes appears!'

Lola poured her some coffee and the two women sat down at the breakfast bar.

'Geraint not here?' enquired Triss as she took a sip.

Lola's cup never reached her mouth; it was banged down on the saucer and then her mouth started to wobble and to her absolute horror she began to cry.

Triss was on her feet immediately. She put a comforting arm around Lola's shaking shoulders and squeezed her. 'Please don't cry, Lola,' she begged. 'Tell me what's wrong. Maybe I can help. It's Geraint, isn't it?'

'Y-yes!' sobbed Lola as she scrubbed at her eyes with a crumpled-up piece of kitchen roll.

'Do you want to tell me about it?'

Lola shook her head distractedly, forcing herself to take deep breaths in an attempt to regain her composure. How could she tell *anyone* what had really happened? How could she reveal that she had been bedded by Geraint solely because he had been angry about the treatment meted out to his sister? Whilst *she* had been harbouring the sad little delusion that he actually *cared* for her!

'I c-can't tell you,' she stumblingly explained. 'It's just too... too...' 'Humiliating' was the word she was groping for, but she couldn't quite bring herself to say it.

'Shh,' soothed Triss, as gently as if she had been talking to Simon, and she began to stroke Lola's arm in a rhythmical way which was oddly comforting. 'It doesn't matter,' she said, in her low, husky voice. 'You don't need to explain anything to me. But if you need an objective ear, or a shoulder to cry on, then I'm always here to listen.'

Her beautiful mouth turned down at the corners and her huge eyes glittered furiously. 'Believe me when I tell you that I am very experienced in dealing with men—especially wayward ones! I've had tons of practice with Simon's father, for example,' she finished on a grim note.

'Wh-who *is* Simon's father?' queried Lola tentatively. 'Or shouldn't I ask?'

Triss's mouth tensed as she shrugged her slim shoulders in a nonchalant gesture which didn't quite come off. 'Can you keep it to yourself?'

Lola nodded. 'Cross my heart.'

'It's Cormack Casey,' said Triss. 'He's the father.'

'Cormack *Casey*?' queried Lola incredulously. 'The Irish scriptwriter?'

'Yes. Mr Hollywood himself,' said Triss bitterly. She gripped Lola's forearm so hard that Lola had to force herself not to wince. 'You won't tell *anyone*, will you, Lola? Please? Apart from Geraint, of course—it's obvious you would tell him—but I don't want anyone else to know.'

'Of course I won't tell anyone,' Lola said. And she certainly wasn't going to tell that smug Welsh swine *anything* she thought! 'It was very good of you to come by,' she said politely, and then a thought occurred to her. 'Was it just to see *me*?'

Triss shot her an understanding look, as though she was quite used to having her motives questioned—one of the banes of being beautiful was that other women always assumed that you were after *their* men. 'Well, I certainly didn't come to see Geraint, if that's what you're wondering!' She sighed. 'I was under the impression that he was rather keen on *you*—'

'Oh, no!' Lola told her quickly. 'He's just a consummate actor, that's all.'

'Are you sure?' asked Triss quietly.

'I'm positive. Whatever there was between us is over now.'

'Oh.' Triss sipped at her coffee thoughtfully. 'So what do you do next—apart from cry yourself stupid, I mean?'

Lola heard the admonishment in the model's voice and managed a watery smile. 'You mean I'm behaving like a wimp?'

Triss shrugged. 'Well, yes—if you want my honest opinion. Why go to pieces? If he comes back—'

'He won't come back!'

Triss ignored that. 'If he comes back and sees you looking all blotchy and down-hearted it will feed his arrogant masculine ego no end, and not do *your* reputation any good in the meantime! Let him look at you and wonder how on earth he could have been mad enough to let you go!'

'How?'

'Well, you could start by changing out of that grotty old skirt and jumper. Make yourself *look* good—'

'But he *won't* come back—I know he won't!'

'And then you'll *feel* good,' continued Triss, as if Lola hadn't spoken. 'And that's the most important thing: how *you* feel—not him! And then you won't *want* him to come back!'

Lola smiled as insurrection stirred in her heart. 'Maybe you're right,' she agreed softly.

'That's better!' Triss finished off the last of her coffee and then gave Lola a pleading look. 'Now—has that helped at all?'

Lola nodded, slightly amazed at how her mood had suddenly lifted so dramatically. 'Yes! It has!'

'Good.' Triss glanced down quickly at Simon, who had begun to stir one chubby arm and now appeared to be trying to scratch his nose with it. 'Because I think you can help *me*, Lola!'

The following day, things looked decidedly rosier for Lola after she had given Simon his lunch and he was happily sitting on her living-room floor banging a wooden spoon hard against a saucepan.

Outside the sun was shining and the mad March wind had gone away, to be replaced by a gentle breeze. Perfect weather for a walk, Lola thought as she screwed up her nose in the way which had had Simon giggling hysterically all morning.

She bundled him into his woolly hat, his coat and his mittens, put him in his pram and then wheeled him outside, her eyes narrowing slightly against the watery paleness of the early spring sunshine.

She walked him round and round the grounds of Marchwood House, listening to the sound of birdsong and doing her utmost not to let her thoughts dwell on Geraint, but without very much success.

She also found herself thinking about Catrin, and Peter, and remembering the day when the news of her inheritance had arrived, like a bolt from the blue.

Lola had thought at first that there must have been some kind of clerical error. Virtual strangers did not leave you mansions worth a million pounds, did they? And she had said as much to the solicitor's clerk.

But apparently they did. And apparently they were also well within their rights not to give a reason for their astonishing generosity. Even to the beneficiary.

The young solicitor had shrugged apologetically when Lola had demanded to know just *why* Peter Featherstone had made his staggering bequest. 'Mr Featherstone wished his reasons for bestowing the gift to remain confidential—and that *is* one of the conditions of the bequest, Miss Hennessy.'

He had given her his bland, solicitor's smile, but the rather insulting glint in his eyes had left Lola in no doubt as to why *he* believed she had been left the house!

He had obviously jumped to the very same conclusion as Geraint, thought Lola bitterly as she bumped the pram across the sunlit lawn and down towards the fountain, where a finely carved wooden seat was placed so that the sitter could listen to the gentle, comforting sounds of the nearby water.

Simon gurgled happily and Lola sat down on the seat, absently rocking the pram, the sun warm on her face, her eyes closed as she drifted in and out of coherent thought, her fatigue presumably brought on by her waking up through the night on the hour, every hour, thinking of that devious Welshman!

Oh, and the torrent of conflicting emotions which seemed to have been raging through her ever since Geraint had first walked into her life—that might also have had something to do with her tiredness, she thought wryly.

She heard no footfall on the still damp grass, had no indication whatsoever that she had a visitor until a shadow blotted the sun from her face and she opened her eyes to find Geraint towering over her, an uncompromising expression darkening his already shadowed features.

Lola's heart fluttered more than her eyelashes and she could have kicked herself for her instinctive re-action, immediately fixing an unwelcoming expression onto her face.

'What do you want?' she asked him ungraciously.

'To talk to you,' he answered grimly.

'I think we've said just about everything there is to say.'

'I think not,' came the unyielding reply.

'You're trespassing,' she pointed out. 'I could call the police and have you thrown off my land.'

'I doubt it,' he answered, with an obdurate smile. 'I could have you in my arms and in bed before you had dialled the first digit! Couldn't I, Lola?'

'How *dare* you?' she questioned furiously, even though her heart was beating like a drum with excitement.

He smiled again, a wicked, foxy smile which made Lola want to scream aloud—he looked so damned gorgeous! 'Is that a challenge?' he asked softly.

'No, it jolly well isn't!'

His grey eyes swivelled in the direction of the pram. 'Why have you got Triss's baby?'

'She's got man trouble,' said Lola, scowling at him indignantly as though *he* were responsible. 'She wanted to be child-free while she tried to sort something out. She's coming back for him later on.'

'Good.' He sat down on the seat beside her and stretched out his long legs. 'Did you miss me?'

'Like a hole in the head!'

'No, seriously.'

Lola turned to survey him with incredulous eyes. 'Good heavens—I actually think you *mean* that!' she exclaimed. 'Why *should* I miss you, Geraint?'

He gave a small nod, like a man who was satisfied with the answer, and then smiled. 'We'll return to that later, Lola—but in the meantime I have several things I need to say to you.'

In spite of feeling that what she *ought* to do was to insist that he leave her property immediately, Lola was intrigued.

'Is Simon warm enough, do you think?' he enquired solicitously as he peered down into the pram.

Lola nodded. 'He's well wrapped up—and the fresh air will do him good.'

'You like babies, don't you?'

'Yes,' Lola agreed, if a little defensively. 'What's wrong with that?'

'Nothing,' he said quietly. 'Nothing at all.' And his grey eyes searched her face.

Well, she was *not* going to enlighten him! Let him squirm! Let him suffer! Let him think she *was* pregnant! That might make him reconsider next time he bedded a woman as some kind of attempt at retribution!

'Say what it is you have to say, Geraint,' she told him bluntly.

'I know why Peter left you the house—'

'So you told me,' she interrupted cuttingly, her voice absolutely dripping with sarcasm. 'Wasn't it to do with my loose morals? Oh, no! I forgot! We disproved that theory with your surprise discovery of my virginity!'

'That's enough!' he ground out.

'But why are you looking so uncomfortable, Geraint?' Lola turned her big blue eyes on him in a mock-trusting look. 'After all, I'm only telling the truth!'

He studied her for a moment with a mixture of exasperation and amusement, then suddenly his dark and snarling mood seemed to evaporate. 'Are you going to let me tell you my story?' he queried silkily.

The trouble was that she was dying to hear it— and, what was more, Geraint knew it, too! 'I can't very well *stop* you, can I?' she snapped.

He hesitated, as if searching for the most diplomatic way of saying it, and that brief temporising was enough to make Lola sit up. Literally. She stared at him, sensing that something momentous was about to happen.

'Please tell me.'

'Peter Featherstone was your father,' he told her gently.

Her denial was instant and furious—what an absolutely absurd thing to say! Her father had died when she was eleven—he was lying!

'No! He was *not* my father!' She was on him in seconds, pummelling her fists hard against his chest, raining blows on him which would have winded a lesser man, but he did not move out of her line of fire, not once; he just let her get her anger out of her system.

'You're lying, Geraint Howell-Williams!' she gasped. 'You're lying to me!'

And then, quite suddenly, all the fight went out of her. She stopped hitting him and slumped back against the bench, like a puppet whose strings had just been cut off.

He spoke calmly, with the solicitude of a doctor breaking bad news. 'I'm not lying, Lola,' he said, very quietly. 'But you know that in your heart. Don't you?'

She buried her face in her hands and rocked backwards and forwards. She did not make a single sound, but when she looked up her cheeks were pale and tear-stained, and pain darkened Geraint's grey eyes as he registered her shock.

'Don't you?' he repeated.

She nodded. 'There's no reason for you to lie, Geraint. I believe you.' Strangely enough, she would have believed him anyway—simply on account of the truthful intensity which burned in his eyes—but there was no need for him to know that.

Not yet, anyway.

'How—did you find out?' she asked eventually.

'I went to see your mother.'

'You've *seen* my mother?' she asked him in disbelief. 'Where? When?'

'Yesterday. I went to Cornwall.'

'But how on earth did you know where she lived?'

'You told me. When we were in Rome. Remember?'

Yes, come to mention it she *did* recollect mentioning the name of the small village in passing. Fancy him remembering that! Lola lifted her head slowly. 'But why did my mother tell *you*?' she whispered. 'And why *now*?'

He looked at her steadily. 'I think that the burden of the secret she's been carrying for all these years finally became too onerous for her to bear any longer—'

'But why tell *you*, Geraint?' she asked him again. 'A man who is a total stranger to her?'

He gave her a soft smile. 'Maybe your mother has more perceptiveness than you give her credit for,' he answered obscurely. 'But perhaps you should ask her for yourself, Lola.'

Lola screwed her face up. 'What? You mean go down to Cornwall? To see her?'

He smiled. 'See her, certainly. But there isn't any need to go down to Cornwall. Why don't you try next door?'

'*Next door?*'

'Uh-huh. I brought your mother back with me. She's at Dominic's. And she's waiting for you, Lola.'

CHAPTER NINE

DOMINIC DASHWOOD'S house, although about four times the size of Marchwood, was nothing like Lola had imagined it would be.

Because he was so rich—richer by reputation than anyone else she knew—she had been convinced that the place would be filled with costly antiques. But it wasn't. It was a minimalist's heaven, with its streamlined, carefully chosen pieces of furniture and its pale, polished wooden floors, occasionally strewn with silk rugs far too beautiful to walk on.

And in the midst of all this understated wealth sat Lola's mother, June Hennessy, desperately trying not to look nervous and failing spectacularly.

She was a woman whose youthful prettiness had survived, to give her face something approaching a serene kind of beauty in her forties. Her ash-blonde hair was still glossy and her beautiful pale blue eyes owed much to her Austrian parentage.

Sitting opposite her now, Lola was taken aback by how different she and her mother looked—and how she had always subconsciously pushed those differences to the back of her mind. She was also still reeling from the fact that Geraint had managed to get her mother up from Cornwall at such short notice, and seemingly without any trouble at all—the man *must* have hidden strengths!

'Will you tell me the whole story, Mum?' she asked as she sat down on a squashy white sofa, her hands locked tightly together in her lap. 'Every bit of it, please. Don't spare me details just because they might hurt me—I *need* to know, you see.'

'Yes, I realise that now,' said her mother slowly. 'Geraint made me realise that.'

Geraint? Why on earth had her mother's voice softened to speak of Geraint in an almost awe-filled way?

But that was not important now. She had come to talk about her father, and Geraint could wait. Lola lifted her chin expectantly.

'Tell me, Mum.'

'It's a story as old as time itself,' her mother began quietly. 'I was just eighteen when I met Peter Featherstone—I was working as a barmaid at the local yacht club and he was taking an extended sailing holiday after pulling off the biggest merger of his career.'

Her smile was tinged with nostalgia as she looked across the room at her daughter. 'He was just over twenty years older than me—but he certainly didn't look it. Or act it! He was a devastatingly handsome man—with dark, curly hair and bright blue eyes just like yours! And he was quite unlike anyone I had ever met before—funny, good-looking, rich and confident. I fell madly in love with him, and, being thoroughly inexperienced, made no attempt whatsoever to hide it. He didn't want to have anything to do with me, of course, not in that way.'

'He—didn't?' asked Lola in surprise.

Her mother shook her ash-blonde head. 'Of course he didn't! I was too young. Much too young. And gauche. Naïve, too. I was looking for Mr Right, and *he* certainly didn't fit the bill—or so he told me!'

'He *told* you that?' asked Lola breathlessly.

'Yes, he did. Peter had never married because he recognised the limitations of marriage—for him, anyway. He told me all this quite honestly—and although it was not what I wanted to hear—I always respected him for his openness.'

'But you had his *baby*, Mum?' said Lola, her brow furrowed with confusion. '*How*—if he was so against it? What made him change his mind?'

Her mother threw her an odd look. 'This part of the story, too, lacks originality. That's one of the things you discover as you grow older, Lola— that patterns of behaviour carry on repeating themselves, no matter how often they fly in the face of experience—'

'Mum, *please*.'

June Hennessy smiled. 'It was the night of the yacht club ball—a *very* prestigious affair—and I was to be Peter's partner.'

'How come?'

'Oh, I had dropped so many hints I think he was too much of a gentleman to say no! And he was planning to leave the following day. I think he thought that no harm could be done on that final evening...which just goes to prove how wrong you can be.'

Her mother's pale eyes took on a far-away look. 'The combination of a dress which revealed far too much cleavage together with the champagne and the night and the music...' Mrs Hennessy looked at her daughter with a defiant spark in her eyes. 'I'm not proud of what happened that night, Lola, but neither do I regret it. Nor shall I regret it for as long as I live—for Peter demonstrated to me what making love *could* be like.'

'What h-happened?' asked Lola in a low voice.

'Peter left the following day, as planned. I assured him that nothing would happen—indeed I was convinced that nothing would. But three weeks later I discovered I was going to have a baby...'

'*Me,*' breathed Lola.

'You.' Her mother smiled. 'You.'

Mrs Hennessy shrugged. 'What *could* I do? I had no idea where Peter had gone. And times were different then—there was a shame and a stigma attached to having a child out of wedlock. John— the man you *thought* was your father—had been in love with me since we were at school together. I think he was almost pleased that I had gone and got myself pregnant, because it meant that I was vulnerable to his proposal of marriage.'

'And did you—love him?' asked Lola slowly.

'I *grew* to love him. There's a difference, you know. At first I was just grateful for his support and understanding—but he was a good husband and, more importantly, a good father, too. Oh, I never loved him the way I had loved Peter—but then I never expected to. That kind of love doesn't come more than once in a lifetime. But John accepted that.

'And John treated you as his own—something for which I will always be grateful—and he was content with the love I *could* give him. He came to the marriage with only one stipulation...'

Lola suspected that she had already guessed what that stipulation had been. 'And that was?'

'That to all intents and purposes you would be *his* child. You were to be registered in *his* name on the birth certificate.'

'And did Peter never come back?'

June Hennessy gave a smile which was tinged with regret. 'Yes, he did. When you were about six months old, he came to find me. He knew that you were his, of course he did, but I denied it, and he played along with what I wanted. I never wanted to trap Peter into staying, you see. He offered me money to support you, but I never took it. John wouldn't have wanted it, and neither, more importantly, did I.' She paused. 'He went away that night—and I never saw him again.'

Lola stared at a magnificent seascape which dominated one of Dominic Dashwood's immense white walls. 'Why did you never tell me this before, Mum?' she asked quietly.

'For what? To upset John? To make you discontented? All for the sake of a tie which had been broken long ago? Peter never got in touch again—your appearance might have caused complications in *his* life. People change, you know, Lola. What if he had denied all knowledge of you? Wouldn't it have been frustrating for you to learn that you had an immensely rich man for a father, yet for you to have no legal claim to his estate?'

'I wonder why he left me this house?' wondered Lola aloud.

'Perhaps he knew that he was going to die. Perhaps he felt it was time to redress the balance of things—to make amends for having deserted you—even though I gave him no opportunity to do anything other than that.'

'And when Dad died,' Lola ventured, 'did you never think about tracking Peter down then?'

'To live happily ever after, I suppose?' Her mother gave her a small smile. 'I felt a little too old and too tired to believe in fairy tales by that stage in my life. Sometimes it's better to have a dream and to hold onto it in your heart, Lola, rather than see it being crushed by the pressures of life.'

'But when you heard about the inheritance from *me* why didn't you tell me the story *then*? Why keep it secret all this time?'

Mrs Hennessy sighed. 'I was too frightened. And too afraid of what your reaction might be if I told you the whole story. Afraid that you might judge me and find me wanting—afraid that you might be ashamed of your somewhat unconventional parentage.' Her mother reached a hand out. 'Are you angry with me for having kept it from you, darling?'

Lola took the outstretched hand and grasped it firmly. 'How could I be angry with you, Mum? I love you, and you did your best. What more could anyone ask?'

Mrs Hennessy smiled. 'And speaking of love,' she said softly, 'is there anything you want to tell *me*, darling?'

Lola brought her fingertips up to cover her mouth, so that her words were muffled and indistinct, but her mother understood them well enough.

'Can you love someone even though you haven't known them very long, Mum? Can you want someone with a blinding passion even though sometimes they make you so mad you want to hit them? Is it possible to want a man's baby even when you know it would be the worst thing in the world which could happen to you at this time?'

'Yes, yes, and yes,' answered her mother, although she blanched a little at the mention of babies. 'I gather we are now talking about Geraint?' she added drily.

Lola nodded, her eyes wide and confused. 'But his motives for getting to know me were so *wrong*, Mum! He was out seeking revenge.'

Mrs Hennessy shook her blonde head. 'It doesn't matter what his motives *were* when he didn't know you, Lola—what matters is what his motives *became* once he *did* know you! How he behaved towards you. Was he honourable and true?'

And Lola recognised that, yes, he *had* been honourable and true—there was no doubt about that. 'Oh, Mum, I feel so *muddled*!'

'Then go to him. Ask him what he feels, what he *truly* feels.'

'I'm scared . . .'

'And Geraint?' quizzed her mother. 'Don't you think that he could be scared too?'

Lola laughed aloud. 'Geraint? Scared? I don't think so!'

'I *might* be scared, if I thought you might refuse to marry me, Lola,' came a deep voice from behind them, and Lola whirled round to see Geraint holding a wriggling Simon in his arms. The baby was wearing a pair of yellow trousers which clashed horribly with his purple sweatshirt. 'He was sick after you left, so I've changed him. These were the only clothes I could find,' he added, and pulled an expressive face.

Lola blinked. *Geraint*—changing babies? And was her hearing growing defective, or had she just heard him asking her to marry him?

June Hennessy got to her feet, walked quickly across the room and held her arms open to the baby, whereupon Simon gurgled and fastened onto her like a limpet.

'What a friendly baby!' Mrs Hennessy observed automatically. 'Now, you two go away,' she instructed her daughter and Geraint firmly. '*Away!* And don't come back until you've sorted things out one way or another.'

Lola was stricken with a peculiar sense of embarrassment, and could look at neither her mother nor Geraint. In fact, she was pleased when Geraint took her firmly by the arm and propelled her out of the house as if the place were about to be detonated by a bomb.

He did not speak until they were next door again, and he had turned on the gas fire in the small study. Then he sat back on his heels so that the flickering flames cast enigmatic shadows on his finely boned face.

'Can you ever forgive me?' he asked quietly.

'For what?' Lola swallowed. 'For forcing me to confront truths which have lain buried for too long? For making my mother rethink her philosophy and tell me something which perhaps I should have learnt about years ago? Those are things for which I should be thanking you, Geraint, not blaming you.'

'For ever doubting you,' came his quiet response.

'Because you wanted to believe the worst of me?' She shook her dark head. 'Who could blame you for that, or blame Catrin, for that matter?'

But he shook his head. 'No. That's the stupid thing. Catrin never apportioned any blame, Lola—certainly not to you.'

'But I thought—'

'Any suspicions came from me, and me alone. Catrin is an independent woman of the nineties, with her own career and her own life. Peter was just a part of that, I realise that now—and she neither asked for nor wanted anything more. He left her some jewellery and paintings, yes, and Catrin was content with that.'

'Then *why*?' asked Lola, gazing at him with a mystified expression.

'Why seek you out with revenge in mind?' He moved his shoulders restlessly. 'That was just me and my arrogant, masculine pride—although at the time I preferred to see it as me protecting Catrin. In a way, I think I felt that I was helping her—as she had helped me all those long, hard years ago, when she brought me up.

'I needed to know *why* my sister's lover had passed her over to leave the most valuable part of his estate to an unknown young woman. I was seething with the injustice of it all! I don't know what I wanted to do to you, Lola, but the moment I saw you I knew—'

'Knew what?' she prompted, her heart thumping like mad.

'That any vague ideas I'd had of revenge were hopeless, because as soon as I looked into your shining, honest eyes I knew that all I wanted to do was love you.'

'Was *that* all?' She gave a soft, secret smile.

He shook his head. 'No, that wasn't all! I discovered that I wanted to marry you, too. To settle down and give you lots of children. All the things I had never wanted before, and had never imagined myself wanting. And then I realised that the reason I had never wanted them before was because I had never met the right woman.' He lowered his voice. 'Until now.'

Lola's eyes shone with unshed tears as she realised that he was giving voice to words she had never thought she would hear. 'Oh, Geraint,' she whispered.

'My parents' marriage was at the mercy of economics,' he told her gruffly. 'Poverty is no basis for a lifetime of contentment. I think that's what gave me the will to succeed—I was determined never to have to submit to the constraints of not having enough money to support a wife and children.'

Lola blinked, mystified. 'But you're rich—and you have the air of a man who has been rich for a long time. There must have been women who have tempted you into marriage before now.'

He shook his dark head. 'Never!' he contradicted her simply. 'Because, conversely, I needed a woman who would love me even if I had nothing.' His grey eyes were unwavering. 'Would you love me if I had nothing to give you but my heart, Lola Hennessy?'

Just for a moment she treasured that look he gave her, his narrowed eyes betraying a fleeting trace of vulnerability. But then he must have seen the love shining brightly in her eyes, for he grinned and stood up, then took her into his arms and held her very, very tight.

'You know I would,' she whispered huskily, 'my darling Welshman!'

He tipped her chin up with his fingertip. 'And marriage, Lola? I want a good, strong marriage,' he told her. 'And it will be an equal marriage, too— I'm not too proud to cook and to bath babies. How do you feel about that?'

Lola gazed up at him. What could she say? She seemed to have hitched her star to the original masterful man. But *oh*, she wouldn't have it any different!

'Well?' he prompted.

'Yes,' she told him firmly. 'Yes, yes, yes! Yes, I'll marry you, yes, I love you—'

'I'm going to make love to you,' he interrupted with a small groan of desire. 'Right now.'

'We have a baby next door we're supposed to be looking after,' she reminded him in a shaky voice. 'Or had you forgotten?'

'No, I hadn't forgotten.' Geraint made a mental note to have Lola to himself for at least a year after they were married. Unless.... 'Are you pregnant, do you think, sweetheart?' he asked her quietly.

Lola shook her head. 'No,' she said half-regretfully. 'I let you think I might be as a kind of way of getting my own back—to make you worried. Are you very angry, Geraint?'

He smiled at her tenderly. 'Angry? No! Relieved? A bit! Disappointed? A little. But we have years ahead to have our babies, Lola—if that's the way God plans it.'

Lola was so flooded with the feeling of being properly loved that she felt secure enough to confide, 'It wasn't *just* for revenge that I told you I might be pregnant, Geraint.'

His mouth curved. 'Oh?'

'Although I hated what I thought you'd done I simply couldn't resign myself to the thought of never seeing you again. I knew that if you thought there was the remotest possibility of me having a baby it would give you a reason to come back.'

His smile broadened. 'I would have come back anyway, my darling—I didn't need a reason. Do you think anything could have kept me away from you, once I'd found you? I've spent my whole life looking for you, Lola, and I'm never going to let you go.'

'Oh, Geraint,' she sighed, her eyes filling up with tears.

'Shh,' he soothed. 'My only regret is not telling you everything before we made love.'

'You tried,' she whispered.

'Not very hard,' he admitted. 'I was too ensnared by you, too worried that you might refuse ever to see me again if you had an inkling of my original motive.' He glanced at his watch. 'What time did Triss say she was coming back?'

'She didn't, exactly.'

He frowned. 'Then do you think your mother might babysit for an hour or so—especially if I take you all out to dinner later to celebrate our engagement?'

'We could always ask her.' Lola gave him a questioning stare, although the look on his face was enough to make her start to shiver in delicious anticipation. 'Why?'

'Go upstairs and wait for me there,' he instructed, a wicked glint in his eye as he picked up the telephone to punch out the number. 'And in a minute I'll show you *exactly* why.'

'And you, being you, would never consider getting no for an answer, I suppose?' said Lola, over her shoulder.

The darkening of his eyes told its own story. 'Never!' Geraint replied, and he smiled as he began to speak to Lola's mother.

*   *   *   *   *

Look out for KISS AND TELL,
next episode in the *Revenge is Sweet* series
by Sharon Kendrick
*Triss Alexander, beautiful model, loving
mother, with an axe to grind against her
baby's father—Cormack Casey.*
Coming Soon...

shocking pink

THEY WERE ONLY WATCHING...

The mysterious lovers the three girls spied on were engaged in a deadly sexual game no one else was supposed to know about. Especially not Andie and her friends whose curiosity had deepened into a dangerous obsession....

Now fifteen years later, Andie is being watched by someone who won't let her forget the unsolved murder of "Mrs. X" or the sudden disappearance of "Mr. X." And Andie doesn't know who her friends are....

WHAT THEY SAW WAS MURDER.

ERICA SPINDLER

Available in February 1998 at your favorite retail outlet.

 The Brightest Stars in Women's Fiction.™